The Cracks

OTHER WORKS BY ANNE DANDURAND
AVAILABLE IN ENGLISH

Deathly Delights

a novel by
ANNE DANDURAND

TRANSLATED BY
Luise von Flotow

The Mercury Press

Translation assisted by the Canada Council.

This translation was revised and approved by the author.

The publisher gratefully acknowledges the financial assistance of the Canada
Council and the Ontario Arts Council, as well as that of the Ontario Ministry
of Culture and Communications through the Ontario Publishing Centre.

AUTHOR'S NOTE: The painting described on page 102 is the work of Anne-
Cécile Thibeault (acrylic on canvas) entitled: "Portrait de Famille, la mort de
Narcisse" ("Family portrait, the death of Narcissus").

Edited by Beverley Daurio
Author photograph by Josée Lambert
Cover photograph by Kevin Omura
Cover design by Ted Glaszewski

Typeset in Berkeley Book and Gill Sans
Printed and bound in Canada
Printed on acid-free paper

First Printing, September 1992
1 2 3 4 5   96 95 94 93 92

Canadian Cataloguing in Publication Data:

Dandurand, Anne, 1953-
   [Coeur qui craque. English]
   The cracks : a novel
Translation of: Un coeur qui craque.
ISBN 0-920544-93-2
I. Title. II. Title: Coeur qui craque. English.
PS8557.A52C6313 1992   C843'.54   C92-094528-7
PQ3919.2.D35C6313 1992

Represented in Canada by The Literary Press Group
Distributed in Canada by General Publishing

The Mercury Press
137 Birmingham Street,
Stratford, Ontario   Canada N5A 2T1

Life: this troubling lie.
— Antoinette Dutremble, *The Happiness of Little Nothings*

What you're trying to do is create a work of art that is
perfect in itself but still conserves the imperfections, the
fragmented, chaotic, human aspect that characterizes
every personal diary written "à chaud." I don't know if it's
possible.
— Henry Miller to Anaïs Nin, *Letters*

These moments in which a memory or even less is enough
to let you slip out of the world.
— Cioran, *Aveux et Anathèmes (Confessions and Curses)*

You're not worth much if you're not worth a giggle.
— *Quebec saying*

I NEVER really sleep.

Or rather I end up falling asleep for a couple of hours of nightmares, but never before midnight and only after strenuous efforts. Well before dawn I'm up again: it's the anxiety. Sometimes I even think the sun won't make it over the top of the mountain and that the day is already over. At four in the morning, the bars are closed, there's no one to call, what else can I do? Light a cigarette and read? Masturbate and go back to sleep? Are you joking? I write.

When I was in love, I slept even less. I would pretend to doze off to lull my lover, and then observe him with intense adoration: a sleeping face reveals all the innocence hidden deep in the soul, I felt as though I were tearing a piece of skin from life, a bedsore of happiness.

I live by my nose. I can recognize the brand of a cigarette by the smell of its smoke. I know what the neighbours on my landing are cooking, which is not always an advantage. Sometimes in the anonymity of the subway, I am deeply moved by certain smells, some people smell so good they seem to come from a forgotten paradise. They're the lucky ones. The only thing that I find truly frustrating in this era of Asocial Assistance[1] (and quite honestly, there's nothing more incorrect than this term), what really frustrates me is that I have to cut down on my perfume. I wait until life becomes intolerable, I never have to wait too long, and then I blast a tiny drop into the hollow of my left forearm four centimeters above my tattoo, I take little sniffs of it till nightfall. It is a perfume made from white flowers only; if I concentrate I can discern lily of the valley, the only naïve thing I can detect at all in the world these days.

I also forget to eat. Or let's say that when my hunger calls, I don't hear it. Practical, with my paltry welfare cheque. But I drink milk, swallow

---

1. A kind of minimal guaranteed income. In Quebec at one time, an absurd form of discrimination allotted people younger than thirty only one-third of the usual welfare allowance. At present, a welfare recipient has to do twenty hours of unpaid work per week in order to receive their cheque, thus becoming the state's most exploited source of labour.

vitamin c tablets, and smoke three packs of ciga-
rettes a day. All things considered, including how
much time I've spent crying, it's a miracle that I
have a complexion like a snowdrop and haven't
yet died of cancer. I am a miracle that is even less
justified than the others.

The need for truth inside me is so strong it
burns. What I don't understand is that I can't stop
lying. I lie to strangers. Not women: women know
right away. But today for instance, I lied to a guy,
good-looking, friendly (I still have to check that
out, so he's got the benefit of the doubt), anyway,
with him I just couldn't resist, I lied. A completely
useless fib about a theatre production I said I'd
seen when I hadn't. Just like that. For no reason.
I don't understand. It burns inside.

My big sack full of little problems is lightened
by almost anything. A misleading clarity in the
winter sky. My cat purring. A second hot bath on
the same day. A painting glimpsed in a gallery
window. The aroma of fresh bread from a bakery.
Little nothings, which is not really so bad.

There's such an emptiness in my belly.

Maybe I'm just endlessly asleep. Maybe I never
woke up.

I can feel that someone is going to come. I don't know who. I'm waiting.

◆

SINCE NOBODY CAME, I'll carry on. I'm used to talking to myself because I'm used to being alone. I'm not complaining: it was hell every time I was a couple. Now it's a little like purgatory, I prefer it to hell, it's cooler and anything is possible.

Today I went to the subway level of Les Atriums.[2] I call it my "think-tank" as though I were going there to think, while it's the exact opposite, it lets me not think. Besides, it's not a tank at all, it's a real jungle redolent with green; anyway it gives me time to stop trying to decipher my contradictions. So, after a twenty minute trip in a subway low on oxygen, I'd been smoking my first cigarette for twelve hundred seconds not thinking about anything, or hardly, when two young tramps who weren't dressed warmly enough for the winter stopped beside me, but not to beg.

---

2. A complex of boutiques in Montreal, characterized by its glass walls, fake jungle, pools and artificial waterfalls.

Usually I just have to stick my head out the door to have someone ask for a quarter, or directions, or want to tell me their problems, doubtless because I don't keep my eyes down like most of the population, anyway they didn't notice me at all and the one said to the other, "Is he there?"

The other one answered, "Yup, there he is in the corner, look, he knows me."

I wanted to know who he was talking about: he was pointing to a corpulent motionless goldfish in the basin strewn with blackened pennies, a completely white goldfish, an albino goldfish.

I said to myself that all over the world the outcasts recognize each other. And then I concluded that with time I had perhaps grown invisible. Or perhaps just this afternoon. I don't know.

◆

A DREAM. I'm in a room with only a deep bed and tangled dark rose sheets, and I'm pressed up against an open window covered by a screen. There's a porcelain sky outside, above a city in ruins, like the Berlin you see in archival films from after the Second World War. I turn toward the bed where a dark-haired man with turquoise eyes is stretched out wearing only a pair of mauve trousers. His chest invites caresses that sparkle, I know this man loves me and I love him, and he's trying to calm me down, whispering, "Don't get so upset, the whole country's like that." I'm still looking out the window, wondering whether the screen is strong enough to stop rats from entering the room; then I whistle a melody by Nino Rota, a lazy little tune.

I'm not really awake, I like this unclear zone between sleep and consciousness; through my eyelids I can feel the sun already high, I hear the jack-hammers at work eighteen stories below my balcony. Lucky today: my anxiety let me sleep till almost eight o'clock! But Chapter Two, my grey cat, is pitilessly walking across my back, ordering breakfast. Good morning, real world.

Today it's not January 19 for me, it's the eleventh day after.

She would have been called Gabrielle.

He would have been called Gabriel.

I overheat, I don't have a humidifier, which is bad for my asthma, I am immodest like most hermits, I'm always naked at home, unless I'm writing. After I checked through the peephole to make sure there was no one in the corridor, I picked up *La Presse*; *Le Devoir* doesn't make it up the elevator, *Le Devoir* waits for me in the entrance. I've tried to understand this, but I still don't know why.

I ran a hot bath with two handfuls of salt and some powdered milk, and emptied a bottle of English blackcurrant bath oil that perfumed the bathroom for hours; since it was a birthday present from Pierre-Pierre in November (frankly bath oil is not sign of love), I was not unhappy to finish it off: one less sign of him in my apartment. Not in me, but I've resigned myself to that: I have a heart made of nylon that can stretch to inordinate proportions; there will always be room for another rip in it. Fortunately. To be precise: my heart is a nylon stocking full of holes, and runs. The comparison came to me when I read in the paper today that nylon is fifty years old while I'm only thirty-four, not so bad, not so bad at all.

I got dressed in blue and black, winter sky and summer night, that's how I feel. I swallowed my theophyline and my five hundred milligrams of vitamin c with some milk straight out of the carton, hello James Dean; then I had some pear juice, such a calm, voluptuous taste, in a flesh-coloured flute glass... happiness manifests itself in the tiniest details.

Like I did yesterday, and will tomorrow, I sat down in my armchair: on my left, my eighty-five dolls observe me impassively with their glass eyes, on my right, the glowing screen of my computer is watching. Where is my truth?: in the illegible and whining scrawl of my private journal from which, a few times a year, the aromatic sapphire of a short phrase emerges? Or here, in the patient labour of stringing together tiny word pearls? Does my truth need to choose between sapphires and pearls?

Today is not January 19 for me, it's the eleventh day after.

She would have been called Gabrielle.

He would have been called Gabriel.

She/he would have had thick soft hair, the dark gaze of moonless summer nights, and a limpid smile. It's all so sad. All of it.

When you think about it, though, the vacuum is not such a bad idea. I'm not talking about mine which doesn't work and is pining away in the purgatory of the broom cupboard; no, I'm talking about the vacuum-for-your-belly like they have at Dr. Morgentaler's clinic. Eleven days ago the nurse was really kind, she had eyes like the sky in my dream, eyes ready to burst, she was holding my hand, I felt like crying, but as in any operation, I was inhaling laughing gas, erupting with laughter, that's me all right, erupting with laughter in a funeral parlour. Gabrielle, Gabriel, poor baby that'll never be more than an angel, my rivers of tears came earlier, for weeks before and you cried with me, in me, when I had to admit that Pierre-Pierre didn't love me, or us. We did a lot of crying, but that's over now, it's sad, you're my biggest wound now, but then you never really know, I've not lost hope that you may come back one day. Gabrielle, Gabriel, I won't cuddle you right away, maybe later, you never know. I don't know.

◆

STILL NOBODY.

Life in Siberia is a serious punishment for political crimes; here it's just another winter. What are the families guilty of whose houses burn down because rats have gnawed at old electrical wiring? What are the friends of the albino fish guilty of? And me, with my two pairs of thick socks, my fur coat that is thirteen years old and still like new, and the apartment I overheat because the heating is included in the rent, I'm not innocent of anything, absolutely nothing, why am I exempt from the general punishment?

No one came yesterday either, but the temperature went up by about thirty degrees, and so we were granted a beautifully rainy 1° Celsius; I thought for a minute that overnight the whole city had moved to Vancouver, but when neither the Pacific nor the Rockies arrived for the meeting in the morning, I gathered that we were benefitting from a short reduction of our sentence. Thanks all the same, but why?

◆

TODAY IS SUNDAY, and I'm listening to religious music on the radio, I've had no gods for some time now except music— rock, jazz and classical. If I hadn't had music resonating during my heartbreaks, I would have committed suicide, I think.

Can anyone explain the consolation in the music of the Stones, Brahms and Miles Davis?

Before, in the Pierre-Paul era, I hated Sundays. During the last act of our relationship I stayed in bed all day, on principle, to protest the very existence of Sundays. I buried myself under the weekend editions of newspapers, monthly journals, scratchy biscuit crumbs and cigarette ashes, only Uproar, the cat I had then, was able to lure me out. I would read a little, go soak a while in bathwater that never had the time to grow cold, AND SLEEP A LOT. Come to write of it, while the Pierre-Paul melodrama was in constant rerun, especially during the last two years when things were really bad, I slept all the time: if I had two working hours a day, it was due to lightened depression and intensified sun, unavoidable.

Don't go thinking that my insomnia now is a sign of serenity, life is more Machiavellian than that.

What amazes me is the kind of armistice I feel inside when I spent twenty years in a black rage; it feels funny, I liked being angry, I thought anger was a sign of vitality and endowed me with cataclysmic energy; when it wasn't caused by the heartlessness of my lovers, it was the condition of the world in the morning papers or the poverty round about that would slap me in the face as soon as I stuck it out the door. But now I'm tired, I would like just a little tranquility, I spent a lot of time revitalizing the office of revolutions, and it seems that if I could just trot along on the luminous path of happiness it would be a good form of repayment, not bad, not bad at all. I'm sure that afterwards I could disinter strength to struggle for disarmament, Ethiopia, the homeless, and giving up smoking. (First things first, as Violette would say, a woman whom I show what I write; I don't know why I like her, maybe it's because she looks like a good fairy.[3])

---

3. There I go again telling lies. I know exactly why I like Violette. First of all, she's the one who contacted me six months ago because she read one of my stories in a literary magazine. She wanted to show me what she was writing. It wasn't much, hardly ten pages; but a month later, Violette's prose was still whirling around in me. We became friends through literature, that's already something solid.

And then what really cemented our relationship was when she came with me to Dr. Morgentaler's clinic. After I'd survived the

Anyway, that Sunday I went for a walk in the
wet snow, down to the east side, the gay
neighbourhood, which isn't really gay, where I
lived at the time of Pierre-Paul. I walked just to
try to forget, just to try and breathe in the cold of
the moment, it required considerable effort but
only for lack of practise. I talked to a woman who
knew me: Anémone, I didn't recognize her, she
has red hair, moss-green eyes and a peculiar
clown-nose, she invited me to visit her, I'll go later
on this week. I have nothing more to lose anyway.
Not even my time.

---

stirrups and the vacuum, and a cramp was twisting my gut into a
triple-shank knot, she told me about when her oldest daughter,
Mélisse, was born. I still don't know why but it was a consolation
for me and for the woman in the other bed who was producing
a flood of tears enormous enough to raise fears of a possible
drowning. That woman, too poor with her five children and
husband-on-the-dole, had made the trip from her village in New
Brunswick on her own. There's no Morgentaler clinic down
there. With one hand Violette was stroking the foot of the
woman from New Brunswick, and with the other, my head. All
that linked us closely together, Violette and me, forever.

◆

I'M TRYING, on the one hand, to imitate a monstrously large iris about to open to the light, and on the other to incinerate my corpses, actually I'm just in the process of acquiring a certain calm. And then Pierre-Pierre phones in a contrite and depressed little voice to say he's got work for me, almost nothing to do for twice as much as my Asocial Assistance cheque, money under the table so I won't lose anything. Oh! There's someone who knows how to get at me. Oh! I was very casual with him, very distant, almost in Siberia, and I said, "Well! All right," and even devised a way to avoid seeing him, at least until next weekend; and immediately afterwards I called my mother, Marguerite, to tell her about the proposal, and then Violette... and played them both the same scene: "Pierre-Pierre is not going to do it to me again, oh no! he's just testing, that's all, it's understandable with a woman like me, no no no, it doesn't bother me a hair, or an eyelash, or a comma... no no no it's nothing, really." Then an hour goes by, and the palms of my hands are moist, and my soul is like a lake in a storm, it's the fear, the cineramasize terror, why is my heart so deaf, so blind, so stupid???!!!!

Oh, oh, oh! I'll have to repeat to myself: he-said-he-didn't-love-me-and-never-loved-me-so-I-do n't-love-him-any-more, it'll be a priceless mantra over the next week.

◆

I'VE DECIDED to move, living on the west side, on the border with the English isn't good for my budget or my mental health, it makes no difference that I'm perfectly bilingual, I just can't stand the feeling that I'm in a foreign city, particularly when I'm in the one where I was born; and so I called Valériane, the sister of one of my actress friends, Dahlia. Valériane was my neighbour during the Pierre-Paul period, she doesn't know it but (along with the music) she once already saved my life with her humour, in other words, I know I can count on her. And sure enough, bingo: the apartment right next to hers is for rent, it's sunnier and cheaper than this place, and roomier, a "modest dwelling" (as my mother, Marguerite, who's careful with language, would say), no stench of tears yet, at least not of mine. The countdown has started, about eight hundred and forty hours plus a few before take-off.

I went for a coffee in the neighbourhood of the promised land. On the way back I ran into R'Erpie on the street, a Ugandan I slept with two or three times, a while ago, chubby type, but wearing the dark suit of the big international reporter, with the crooked legs of a rachitic childhood and a Master's in poli sci from the Sorbonne. To flatter me, he'd always mutter: "You know, you're the queen of intimate destabilization," anyway, the most rigid prick of my entire past, the sexual technique of a pile-driver and a heart whose size was in keeping with my thin little figure; but when tenderness misses the train, I tire of things very quickly, but since there was no blood between us, not even tears, we always meet with the complicit smile of those who have let a few tigers growl under the sheets; so I wasn't able to lie to him and I summarized my most recent tragedy (it's not because I spread every little detail out here meticulously like the last bits of peanut butter on the last slice of bread the day before my Asocial Assistance cheque arrives, that I can't synthesize the situation in a conversation), anyway, do you know what he said, a cliché fat as his arm— wait a minute, I'm letting him get to me— impressive as a baobab (and it slipped easily out of his mouth as though every journalist harboured a herd of banalities he can let loose). He eructated, "You are just too whole, you frighten men off."

From which I concluded:

a) that I was right to end everything with him;

b) that if that's the price to pay for love, I'll have very little, thank you very much: one of the things I find most depressing is the meat counter at the supermarket.

Later, I was leaning against the post at a bus stop waiting for a bus that was as slow in coming as hope and the month of May, engrossed in my book on butterflies instead of the book on glacier formation I read in the summer. Anyway, I didn't feel a thing until a cherubim touched me on the shoulder. He had an awful face, the look of a tramp or someone released prematurely from the asylum, his red hair gummy with dirt, his lower lip split open and bleeding, but with eyes light grey as the universe before dawn. He stayed there for a long time, with his face close to mine, and ended up softly murmuring, "Yes."

Just yes.

I swear on everything I have that is precious— it's not much but it's important to me— the cherubim disappeared immediately after.

I missed the bus because I was desperately trying to figure out what to say yes to.

◆

THE TIME HAS COME to make some confessions: I was telling a lie when I wrote that I always look through the peephole of the door before I pick up my newspaper. That's only half-true: half the time I don't bother. This morning my next-door neighbour caught me. His apartment always smells of bourgeois French cuisine, his wife has lost all her hair (I suspect it's through chemotherapy, if I dared I'd offer her a joint, it's supposed to reduce the nausea), and they cohabit with a gigantic mastiff. Usually I hear him rattle his chain in front of my door, but this morning the husband was alone. So, since I didn't hear the chain, my neighbour saw me completely naked. But he kept right on going, either he's a perfect gentleman, or he was momentarily struck by blindness (an illness more frequent than you think), or my level of morning invisibility is very very high.

I was also lying when I wrote that I am always completely alone: if you count all the nameless people out on the street who talk to me, and the not negligible number of women friends I have, I am very popular. More precisely though, I feel alone because I sleep alone, when I sleep. And don't go thinking I'm complaining; since I felt even more alone than alone when I was a couple, I don't think there's a solution. Except, perhaps, to laugh about it, and then you have to want to. So, things could be worse.

In order to counteract the invisibility factor, I went to see Anémone, on foot, seeing as either the greenhouse effect or Chernobyl was making the winter grimace under the mocking mask of a hasty spring.

If you could only see her house, a wonder, all in wood, and light as a river before pollution, vast enough for four generations of Muscovites, if it were located in the USSR. And it hardly costs her anything, because it's a cooperative. I don't know if Anémone appreciates her luck, she probably does because she's got her head on straight, or almost.

She reminded me of how we met: on a flight to Paris about twelve years ago. I can't really remember her, at the time I was just an actress, completely dishonest with the entire world, every month I blew at least two or three times my current Asocial Assistance on exclusive and expensive dresses, I told nothing but lies during working hours, and thought only about suicide, but no one would ever have guessed: I maintained superb form, smiling and invulnerable, inside I weighed a ton all told while outside I was splendidly anorexic.

And Anémone was a brunette at the time.

There we were going over her memories when a guy still half-asleep wandered into the kitchen. She introduced him as the love of her life, Rocky Chiasson. I suppose he may be able to kindle love at first sight in some people, in spite of his growing baldness and his ordinary brown eyes. But his two-faced wanker's smile à la Baby Doc made me slot him as a repulsive speciman, size extra-large. I didn't say a thing, I keep my comments for my writing, you would never believe how uncommunicative I am in everyday life. But I'll be back to visit Anémone, she may need me one of these days.

On the way home I made a detour to go see Violette, nothing really moves me except anxiety and death, and even with those two I don't let things make too great an impression on me, it's a question of habit. Anyway, I really needed to have a laugh with Violette but it wasn't the right moment. She was in an icy rage, even worse than the winter temperatures today, worse than the Antarctic.

Her neighbour, a creep I have the honour not to know, had come to see her earlier in the day to spout off about having ejaculated in a dream he had about fucking Gentiane, Violette's youngest daughter, a child who proves beyond all doubt that beauty is still a possibility down here. A dream is fair enough, it's no more controllable than American military spending, but showing off with it... that makes you want to vomit.

Violette concluded: "Kids are the only pure thing left in this cesspit of a twentieth century, with a sicko like that pig over there I can see how electric shock treatments might be useful." I shared her opinion, of course.

The balance of the day: a momentarily blind neighbour, a reject that would perhaps need some stepping on, and a piece of garbage to be closely observed, if not eliminated...

Can't wait for tomorrow.

As if that will change anything.

◆

A NEW WEEK HAS BEGUN, I say that as though the other one had come to an end, which is not really true, it's continuing, I hardly have time to breathe, let alone write. To summarize my meeting with Pierre-Pierre yesterday: I didn't suffer. Not at all. I had to review a filmscript he wrote, a violent, seedy, really odious piece. I was just a little afraid I'd be identified as the embittered ex-babe, but luckily, I wasn't the only one who thought it was bad: the producer and the cameraman hired for the same job agreed with me. So the discussion was rather reassuring: my unhappiness hadn't altered my critical capacities.

Outside, it was glacial and sparkling, the way I felt inside facing Pierre-Pierre. Poor guy: it must be pretty hard to put feeling into what you write when you haven't had any in real life for a long time. But basically, I understand him: the heart is a minefield in the twentieth century, mutilated and dangerous at the same time, I can see someone refusing to venture there.

◆

TODAY I DREAMT I had an artificial leg from my left knee down.[4] It had a dainty little cast-iron hook in the shape of a tiny carriage attached to my stump with a miniscule horse. There was an unreal sun in the sky, like in the drawings of children; certain feminists I worked with when I was a journalist also appeared. I detached my fake leg without a fuss, and placed it on the table, thinking, "I'm lovable even if I do have a piece missing." Then a penguin-style man, fortyish, in an English suit that was too perfectly tailored, (the kind of guy I usually have an irresistible urge to spit at),

_____

4. Say, papa Jung, is there any connection to Marguerite's mother who had a leg amputated, and who I loved a lot?

approached me in order to proclaim, "I very much liked your collection of stories, and in particular the line: 'In the sleeping night when my doves are murmuring.'"[5]

Then, still in my dream, I fell asleep with the guy from page 9, the good-looking, nice one (although that hasn't been tested yet, but he does have the benefit of the doubt, remember?) who clasped me tightly against him. He's an Italian with periwinkle eyes who laughs a lot and is quick to fly off the handle. Mamma mia Marguerita, that guy sure has an effect on me....

Inexplicably, I woke up with a formidable craving for sex, a hole in my belly, a crater in my heart, which led me to reconsider my last twenty years of operative sexuality. You can constantly scrutinize your past, but there are certain conclusions that can only be drawn much later, and I suddenly realized that I hadn't had much luck with cunnilingus. Though I perfected the opposite technique

---

5. A note to any future critics: don't go looking through my earlier work, I never wrote that.

with all the discipline of a ballerina (still reserving my best mouthwork for those I really loved), out of all my lovers there were one or two who'd had the elegance to perform cunnilingus, and even that was rare, too rare; and only one had really loved to make me come like that.

Him I remember. I'd gone off with a girl I nicknamed Bad-Boy-Thistle because of her tendency to get together with just anyone. But that time, her Number 44 wasn't so bad, and the three of us took Number 44's convertible and his tent and drove to the Atlantic Coast near Portland.

I love the sea. It doesn't ask any questions. It sings. It doesn't go away. And so I was doing my most expert imitation of the half-dead-body-tossed-up-by-the-waves-and-cultivating-skin-cancer when suddenly, through my salty eyelashes, I noticed a faraway repro-incarnation of the famous Greek god, Pan, a little thinner and without the goat's ass, at least as far as the naked eye could see.

I didn't move, I was reaching catalepsy I felt so good, and a good millenium later I heard a suave voice, a man's voice to boot, purr, "You should take care, you're catching a sunburn."[6]*

Eyes closed I assumed this was some kind of beanpole trying to make conversation. I opened my eyes and discovered Repro-Pan in person, even better-looking close up.

To get to the point, Bad-Boy-Thistle and Number 44 went home three days later. I stayed on for three weeks living the easy life in a new empyrium with Panagiotis, a son of Greek immigrants and a neo-impressionist painter.

In the middle of the forest, about five minutes from the sea, Panagiotis had built a house completely from maple, with stained-glass windows in the roof that cast floods of rainbow light on the bed. Our days and nights were easily filled with the vital minimum: food, oral and genital sex, painting for him, and my journal for me.[7] Add the

---

6. In other words, "Look out, you're reaching the crimson hue of the solar star dropping into the Aegean Sea."

* English in original.

7. Minimum, or rather maximum, in any case anything less than that is only a semblance of life. How many of us here are living-dead?

swell of the sea and the thousands of different
smells from the woods, and I could have submit-
ted to the illusion that my happiness was perfect,
and foolproof.

But illusions don't live long, if at all, something
that is not at all obvious, especially where I'm
concerned: when Panagiotis demanded that I give
up my language, my work, my home town, my
friends and my mother, for him, I said no.

If Repro-Pan could have instantly turned into a
real Zeus, with lightning in his hands to annihilate
me, he would have acted and I would be dead! I
have never seen anyone get into a rage so quickly
and so violently: why did I give myself to him,
then? why was I so shameless? didn't I have any
sense of modesty? In other words he trotted out
all the usual moral arguments in all their usual
repetitive boredom.

I was able to shut his trap by telling him that I
was dying of lung cancer, that I couldn't waste
even a moment's enjoyment, and I added a wealth
of pertinent medical details (to be a really good
liar you have to read the papers), I even sobbed
and coughed with all the despair of the *Dame aux
Camélias*, (one of those moments when it was

essential to be a tragedian), anyway, I left him there in his empyrium of wood with shame in my soul for having let out such a huge lie in self-defense. I could have decamped with just my dignity, but no, I had to save my honour and burden my conscience with another dirty load. Not very bright, really not very bright.

Today, to celebrate Valentine's Day, I tried to remember the last time someone said, "I love you." Since I had to go back almost ten years, I immediately broke down, sobbing like a kettle that is full to the brim and boiling. Every decade I allot myself seven minutes of self-pity. When you've hit rock bottom, there's always a way of digging up presents that are really inexpensive, especially for Valentine's Day.

Since I'd had the dream about the Italian, I ignored my lack of courage and sent him an invitation to the launching of an anthology that included one of my little stories. I sent it anonymously. Hello boldness!

I hope he comes, though, and that one evening, there'll be real love between us, hearts included, that'll last, if possible, till our legs grow wobbly and our hair silver.

(And I hope he'll be good at cunnilingus, to bring up my average.)

Why is it that when you spend years like a tightrope walker over an abyss, and you end up finding it comfortable and even managing to laugh about it, why do you still suddenly become afraid of falling? Why do you want to climb back down, and why do you forget how?

◆

I DIDN'T GO to the book launch, I had a massive fever, a Malaysian jungle in my head, I drank water but unfortunately lost a little more weight. I dreamt of him again, we were exchanging a long kiss full of laughter and flourishes, a rare kiss. Later than usual, but still well before the bulldozers and dynamiters established below arrived, I woke up convulsively muttering, "Leave me alone! It's not my fault! I can't help my nocturnal ecstasies!"

It's getting worse.

To bring myself back down to earth, I put on skeleton earrings and dressed like a gangster in the movies, in black with a white tie. Is there a

Cosa Nostra of the heart, and if so, why was I never contacted?

Since I missed the book launch I decided to go buy his latest book. I got ready; put a Paolo Conte cassette in my Walkman (in my era of tears I couldn't go out into the street, and even less enter the subway, without my Walkman, I was closed down tight to everything that had life energy, and sure that when the Phoenix was reborn, it had earphones on.) But now, if I hear people talking in my vicinity, I cut the sound, poor Paolo Conte is continually fragmented...

I really liked the Italian's book, especially the line: "a pen and its abrasions." For me it would probably be "a keyboard and its wounds," but then I understand the delicacy of euphemism.

Since he talks a lot about his exile, you get involved, especially when you think of all the slush and the more than camouflaged beauty of Brossard.[8] If I ever talk to him, I'll let him know that my country is either:

---

8. A colourless suburb of Montreal.

a) words, with all the attendant obsessions;
or
b) the Absolute. (I've been tracking down the men of my race for some time now, they seem to be getting scarce, or I no longer know how to get in touch.)

If ever I end up alone with him, I'll take off my glasses and my watch, to hell with precision and death, which is always too near; I want to see him in the blurred immortality of a Manet painting.

Look what happens, I give my personal crazy lady just one sprig of hope and she loses control, fills the house with dust particles that panic in the light. Which is all right for me, I prefer dust to ashes.

Serious, very serious.

To relax, I went over to Anémone's, she was as green as her eyes today. Just before I got there she'd laid Tarot cards; sniffling like a rainy day, she said, "Take a look, though, it's a wonderful hand, I don't understand a thing, nothing. Why do I feel so awful?"

I repeated "why?", just "why," and that's when she told me, out of the blue, without a warning, that she'd been menstruating for seven months.

Every day. I asked her if it was just a little, or a lot, or an enormous amount. She said, "An enormous amount." I had a bloody vision of an Annapurna of sanitary pads. Anémone suddenly leant over toward the floor and called, "Chagrin, Chagrin, come here, my sweet."

I thought one of three explanations might apply: either her sadness is hanging around on the floor below the table, or Anémone has a cat that is as invisible as I am at certain times of the day, or more prosaically, the menstrual pain makes her bend double.

But I didn't have the time to decide because— was it by chance or just destiny— Rocky arrived on the scene, wrapped in a sheet in the style of historical films of the fifties, with the smell of sex like a haze around him; he threw himself on Anémone and kissed her voraciously, paying no attention to her washed-out eyes.

I took another note of the fact that I detest the super-vacuousness of his smile, a non-detachable plastic smile. For me, happiness that is indifferent to suffering is lethal; but then Jacinthe appeared behind Rocky, sleepy and just as poor an adaptation of the historic-Roman as the heartthrob. Jacinthe, good old Jacinthe! Blond as the sun in July and a mouth to drive the most virtuous Jehovah's Witness mad. I hadn't seen her since theatre school, a good twelve years.

She is still just as sumptuous, even when she's unkempt, even with her eyelids stuck together, she didn't even notice that Anémone and I were there, I deduced that invisibility is contagious. Jacinthe gulped down a bit of fruit juice and went back to bed in the only bedroom, with Rocky on her heels.

Anémone was pale, her skin colour close to the very gentle green of certain Fragonard paintings, but without the nonchalance.

In a horrible stammer, I said I understood perfectly, "With last night's heavy wet snow, it would have been absolutely insane to send a friend home... It would even have been dangerous: Jacinthe could have slipped and broken a leg, maybe even her hip, a hip takes a long time to heal... And it's proof of friendship, real friendship, to put her up like that in your own bed... "

But Anémone cut short my naïve stutterings, tossing out that Jacinthe is Rocky's mistress and her own too, and that at the moment she was jealous of him and of her, and that it had been going on for seven months.

Seven months of jealousy. Seven months of hemorrhaging. That really blew me away, I couldn't find the words, the good old, ordinary words that calm and console. I left, the pale green and blood-red shoals of love bowl me over, and my ship is already taking water, I'm not eager to go under. Not at all. Not today, anyway.

I wasn't very proud of myself in the subway, powerlessness and guilt tortured me, together their grip was solid. To try to escape from them I helped a blind man who didn't have a dog, I carried the very heavy suitcase of a thin old woman, I gave a poor violinist a quarter, I picked up all the greasy papers rotting away on the platform, I left the twenty-three cigarettes I had on me with the grubbiest tramp. Nothing helped, I was suffocating because I'd refused to help the victim of a concentration camp of the heart, and worse, it was Anémone, it's always worse when you know them. Much worse.

I'll go back to see her. I can't just abandon her like that.

◆

ALL YOU DO is turn a page, and the universe, including my skinny little self, has grown three weeks older, oh the magic of literature. You turn a page, and during this time how many Manuels have died in the mildewed jails of South America, how many Maroussias have suffered hunger and cold in the gulags, how many little Ahmeds have had their fingers crushed by Israeli soldiers? I was thinking about that recently, it stopped me grumbling over the miniscule chaos of my own life.

The chaos was moving house, a primal kind of experience, especially when you think you own absolutely NOTHING, and there are forty boxes in front of you, twenty sacks of clothes, a dozen cases full of illegible manuscripts and a mountain of whatsits, thingammies and more or less identifiable gadgets, in effect it's the weight of the past that you move, and dare not throw out. The hard work was done by the three young movers who emptied my apartment in the time it took me to drag on three cigarettes; free of nostalgia, I listened one last time to the explosions of the excavators below my balcony, during the day it conjured up the atmosphere of Beirut, without the shelling, but still, I thought: goodbye Beirut, and hello, forced labour.

My mother, Marguerite, came to help me but I soon sent her back to her bridge tournaments; as a private Arts Council[9] and with all the fatigue and worry I've caused her, she has already suffered a lot, you mustn't overdo things even with a mother's heart, especially with hers which is too big and no longer very young. My brother Vincent, the most handsome one of the family, who spends the whole year locked away in his dark room, showed me how useful indefatigable youth and the arms of a man can be. My neighbour Valériane served us tea at regular intervals at her place; it was odd to see the two of them sitting across from each other like that, I kept having visions of an apple tree and a cherry tree in full bloom, probably because of the colour of their cheeks.

Chapter Two spent three days sulking under the sink, I can't believe she was feeling homesick

---

9. A federal agency that gives grants to artists, at least to some.

for the English, or the noise of the traffic, or the vertigo of living on the eighteenth floor. No, I think she was meditating on asceticism and a disdain for material possessions, like everyone does who wrecks their back washing down cupboards, moving furniture, attaching shelves, undoing boxes and all the rest of it... but I know us: asceticism and a disdain for material possessions are forgotten the minute you're settled in.

◆

THE FIRST DAY OF SPRING, fragile and radiant as an adolescent putting on make-up for the first time; the Portuguese women of my new neighbourhood would be sweeping the sidewalk in front of their doors, the sun would be trickling down the drainpipes, over the windows and the faces; it would be early afternoon, and walking down the sunny side of the street I would reach the salmon-and-mauve-coloured tea room, order a jasmin tea and a *religieuse* that would melt in my mouth, oh the joy of discerning taste buds; he would come in by chance, and unable to avoid me because I was the only customer, would take a seat nearby, we would first talk literature, but very quickly turn to what we were writing, and who we were. After a few hours the sun would slip behind the madder curtains. With the tip of his fingers, he would touch the inside of my wrist, my heart would leap in a way I no longer thought possible, I would unlock the cubbyhole of my soul and reveal the heap of ashes, he would tell me about the wind and dust in his own country, we would go out, and in the evening drizzle we would not hold hands but walk in the haze of our confidences, and he would only take me into his arms much later, much further on, and I would hope that the moment never wore off.

The next morning, near the newspapers on the doorstep, I, myself— let's say— she would dis-cover a purple orchid in a translucid box, a marvel in the light snow. Every morning afterward, an orchid would be waiting for her, and years later he would still deny that it was his gift, except that every year afterward, on the anniversary of their meeting in the salmon-and-mauve tea room, the same orchid would be smiling at her through the newspapers. That would be the only lie, a most gentle one, of the long life of their love.

He would only have kissed her after a few weeks, time enough for her to patch up her ragged past by recounting it to him, there's nothing like love to heal love's old abrasions. In the heart of a night of rain, in a grayish café transfigured by their presence, she would be the one to suddenly lean toward him for their first kiss, and he would be the one to wish the moment would never fade.

Then, finally, they would have appeared arm in arm in public, in the streets, at the cinema, with no pity for the lonely women, the lonely men, and a whole month would have gone by before, trembling in the rose-coloured bedroom, he removed each piece of clothing for her, and the glorious desire of his body would dazzle her, and she would tear off her flashy gear and come close to him, all of her skin against all of his, he would take her like that, standing in the rose-coloured bedroom that was veering to purple, with purple blood galloping in their veins; then she would cry, from joy, and he with her, because after so many years of darkness their eyes couldn't withstand so much light.

◆

OH, THE EXCESSES of creativity!

That's enough, I quit.

Because of internal burns.

I was cold, I just wanted to warm up. Not end up charred.

Writing as an emotional stimulus for the soul, I don't know if I can allow myself that, seeing as I have a rather pressing need for a miracle ointment.

What I wanted to do was invent their whole lives, my whole life, and even my happy old age, but I'm not the one who decides that.

It's decided for me.

And the decision was that enough is enough, the gap of the conditional.

Except that the present is rather less inspiring.

Twice, a month ago and again last night, I took all my courage into one hand (the left hand, closer to the heart), and the telephone in the other, and invited the Italian to a theatre premiere.

He declined:

a) the first time, because his *nona*— his grandmother, aged ninety-seven years, five

months, twenty-two days and a few hours—
had just expired;
b) last night, because a local poet had just
croaked, and he, the Italian, felt obliged to be
present at the funeral parlour, near the
corpse (who could hardly have cared less).

In his silken voice, the Italian said, "There are
always deaths between you and me."

I added, "Yes, and then there's my dog, I mean
I think my dog is dead."

A moment's silence. Then the Italian's voice,
sounding just a little frayed, said, "Ah? What was
his name?"

The air was laden with salt, and I felt as though
I was on a quay when the steamer casts off; I
breathed, "Don't cry, he never had a name. My
dog just died with you."

The Italian understood, and laughed. I did too.
In conclusion, I did too.

◆

ALL MY INSOMNIA has moved house with me, unfor-
tunately; last night I didn't sleep at all because I
had a terrible longing to run my hands through a

man's hair. No head of hair I already know, thank you very much, instead, hair with an unfamiliar texture, hair that was quite frizzy, closer to wool than flax; to tell you the truth, around four-fifty-one in the morning, I was even able to immerse myself in his smell, a mixture of good male sweat (without any touch of smoke, but still highly suggestive), and a cloud of honeysuckle *eau de toilette* (a perfume in which I always imagine commas and suspension points whirling around).

It makes for a very disturbing sensation in the palm of the hands, this virulent omen of a future-that-can't-get-any-more-hypothetical. Very disturbing, especially when you know nothing, absolutely nothing, about who the hair in question might belong to.

Chapter Two, who is extremely sensitive to the state of my soul, attempted the impossible and deployed all of her fur to replace the head of hair, but the project lay well beyond the capacities of the little sweetheart.

◆

NOTES SCRATCHED into my black notebook in the subway, on the way home:

"Let's just say, sir, that I was very trusting. First of all, it was quite unwise to write to a novelist I didn't know to tell him about my sincere admiration. The problem was that he'd just published his first book, and I'd read a few pages of it in *Le Devoir* which set off this naïve enthusiasm. It was totally unwise, and quite careless to include my address and telephone number at the bottom of my letter— a letter whose style I'd subjected to severe criticism, a point I'd like to stress."

"(...)"

"I know, I know, I shouldn't have. But it was spring, sir, and I don't know if you realize what kind of madness ravages Montreal on the first real day of light and warmth, when people begin to leapfrog over the last dying patches of greyish snow."

"(...)"

"I'm not saying that spring was actually responsible, I'm just trying to establish the facts with the greatest possible accuracy. So, it was on the evening of that day that Crépin Vandégueux first phoned me. Five days ago. I met him in a bar where the beer is cheap and the popcorn free. I was walking with a cane that night."

"(...)"

"Yes, I suffer from a recurring form of sciatica that is very painful, every now and then it comes back and stiffens my left leg, the cane helps me a bit, but I'm also a bit of a show-off, a cane can be so elegant..."

"(...)"

"No, not today, I don't have it with me today...You think that might be a reason?... Or is it my haircut? Do I look like a defenseless child?"

"(...)"

"Well, on the cover of his novel he looks short and fattish, but he's the opposite really; he's the skinny type, almost fleshless, it's the alcohol that's made him swell up, but in any case, he's twice my height and twice my weight..."

"(...)"

"Honestly, sir, I've spent HUNDREDS of hours talking literature with alkies, and even with druggies, without anyone ever trying to... For instance the poet who died two weeks ago, I used to buy him red wine, some Pasolini for the name, and we'd get shamelessly drunk, him and me, all alone in my living room, or his, and he never tried to..."

"(...)"

"Crépin Vandégueux called me back around five-thirty today and invited me over to his place. The odd thing is that I recorded his address on my watch. Look, I have an electronic watch, but the sound is bad: after I hung up I realised I couldn't hear it. I should have taken that as an omen... Instead, I just headed out... trusting my memory. And I had the right address, unfortunately for me..."

"(...)"

"A dump, I'm afraid, almost a caricature, two disgusting rooms you might see in a film about an impoverished young writer and your reaction would be, "Impossible, the set man's exaggerating." First of all, his bed, or rather the filthy mattress, was right behind the entrance door, and all around it the floor was strewn with garbage, absolutely everything, disgusting bits of pizza, blackish engine parts, rusty hubcaps, and beer bottles with cigarette butts inside, of course... It smelled dirty and unaired, of dirty ashtrays and stagnant dishwater..."

"(...)"

"Nothing, sir, there was no foreseeing that... To show you how trusting I was, I didn't tell him a single lie, not one. We gabbed for two hours, nice and calm."

"(...)"

"Yes, of course I tell lies, I can't help it, normally only to men, but NOT to Crépin Vandégueux, unfortunately for me..."

"(...)"

"And not right now either, sir!!! I'd like to remind you that I'm not here for pleasure but by obligation, I would much rather be at the other end of the galaxy tucked under a tuft of phosphorescent lichen!!!"

"(...)"

"Excuse me. I'll go on. We were in what he uses as a kitchen, I was sitting in the only armchair, a sagging wreck."

"(...)"

"When I think about it, sir, maybe. I should tell you that we showed each other what we'd written during the day. It's not really my fault, it really isn't, it's just that I have a computer, anyway it turned out that mine was clearly better than what he'd done. It was sheer accident, sir, because very often what I write is really bad... I remember now that it annoyed him, but at the time I didn't pay any attention. Unfortunately for me..."

"(...)"

"Around seven thirty I wanted to go home. I was tired. I never sleep a lot. It was when I wanted to leave that..."

"(...)"

"You really need the details?"

"(...)"

"Well, here goes. I put my hand on the door handle. Crépin Vandégueux jumped me. Then he threw me to the ground. He flattened me under him. I struggled. I screamed. My head was whirling. I felt a black rage against him. And I was scared. I was Palestine, Negro women under apartheid, Jewish women under Hitler. But those images passed quickly, very quickly, sir, as though in moments like that thoughts want to break the sound barrier, escape the force of gravity. Suddenly my right hand touched a rough metal bar. I swear I didn't stop to think; my right hand closed on it. I stopped moving. It was a crowbar. What was Crépin Vandégueux doing with a crowbar by his bed? Did he use it to scratch his back? Pick his nose? We will never know, sir, because when he let go my right arm to undo his fly, I bashed him hard on the back of the head. Total success: he didn't even gasp."

"(...)"

"I shoved him off me and got up. I was holding on to the crowbar in case one blow wasn't enough. But I soon stopped trembling: the young hopeful of Quebec literature was lying at my feet, his dribbling prick out of his pants and a patch of blood gumming up his awful haircut. Then I called you. When your colleagues arrived I was still holding the crowbar. You never know. That's all."

"(...)"

"He's not dead? Just in a coma? Good. Where do I have to sign? Here? There you go. Can you tell me where the toilets are? I feel sick."

Twenty minutes later, outside the District 34 police station, the night was admirably indifferent to all forms of violence. As usual.

◆

THE NEXT DAY I was in a state of disquieting excite-
ment: I kept repeating to myself that over the
course of my short life I'd been attacked four
times, and that no one had ever got his way. I kept
repeating, "When's the next bout?" Valériane, my
neighbour, came to the conclusion that I was
taking it all rather well. But you should have seen
me the day after. Draped in several layers of
shapeless clothes, I was shivering in spite of the
wonderful softness in the air, the tiniest sound
terrified me. I ran six or seven hot baths, soaping
each centimeter of my skin with the meticulous
care of a surgeon. I guess that if Crépin
Vandégueux had made it, I would have been
scouring myself with bleach, and then the muddy
stream of questions for which there are no an-
swers: why does evil exist? will he kill me when
he comes out of his coma? why me, when all I
want is to be illuminated by beauty, have a spot
or two of tranquility, a little nothing of love, and
then, if possible?... I won't go on, you understand.

Anémone phoned me and before I even had
time to open my mouth she told me about the

weekend of "personal growth" called *Agora* she
spent with Rocky; there were sixty people locked
up in a small windowless room, forbidden to
smoke or leave for a piss; everyone took a turn
sitting out in front on an upright chair and talking
about his or her problems, encouraged by the
chorus of shrieks from the others; they shouted at
Anémone to tell her it was good to be jealous, and
at Rocky that it was good to cheat on her; I ought
to participate in *Agora*, it would do me an incred-
ible amount of good, it only cost four hundred
and twenty-five dollars for two days, and all in all
she was floating in the most complete joy and next
week she and Rocky were getting married: did I
want to come?

I replied:
a) I wasn't going to any more weddings
because all the ones I had attended had
ended up in divorces, so I must be bad luck;
b) I got four hundred and ninety-seven
dollars a month from Asocial Assistance,
which was rather an impediment to my
"personal growth"; I also objected to paying
even a penny to get yelled at, and yesterday
someone tried to rape me which was

absolutely free of charge.

Before she hung up Anémone let me know I was a total cliché with my abortion and my rape.

That crucified me. Seen from this angle then, the morning sun, birthday presents, childhood, suffering, dying, loving, everything, absolutely everything can be reduced to a cliché!

I put Miles Davis' "Tribute to Jack Johnson" on full blast, and huddled under my electric blanket set on high. Compassion, clemency, and I did not feel very powerful, caught in the jaws of the twentieth century.

◆

I DIDN'T GET OFF that easily. A week later I got a heavy-duty asthma attack. It started around eleven o'clock with my breath whistling in every key. Whenever that happens I tell myself this is the scientific explanation for the voices of Saint Joan of Arc. And just like every other time, I waited in vain for things to calm down, they didn't, and by five in the morning I looked about as intelligent as the sunfish on the bottom of Pierre-Pierre's rubber dinghy last summer.

What I like about my hospital is the uproar
when I arrive, even when Emergency is com-
pletely jammed: whack! the wheel chair, whack!
the oxygen mask, whack! the needle into the vein
of my left arm, whack! the solution, whack! a
scarier needle into the artery on my right wrist to
analyse the arterial gas, whack! a course of in-
halotherapy. After a failed attempt to use my
microscopic strength to inhale through a machine
with pistons, I was given the right to "The Cadil-
lac" as the tiny inhalation therapist called it, which
consisted of her administering a great many pow-
erful blows to my upper chest and back in order
to set off a prolonged coughing fit. The connection
between this vigorous treatment and the luxury
vehicle seemed rather obscure: it must be an
example of colourful medical vocabulary, but I
didn't pursue the investigation... there is a time
for semantic inquiries and another for emergen-
cies.

So I took a turn on "The Cadillac" every two
hours with the pretty Emergency doctor nick-
naming me "Blue Raisin" for the colour of my skin
(a gross exaggeration), anyway, there were lots of
jokes for three days and two nights. You may

think I'm telling lies as I write this, but believe me, given the euphoric effects of oxygen and the rattling noises produced in the next room by:

a) the young motorcycle accident victim;

b) the fifty-year-old man with the triple by-pass;

c) the old nun with metastases right through to her bones,

there really was something to joke about, because death wasn't scraping by me quite as closely.

Marguerite, my mother, came for a visit, poor thing, she never even has a cold, so illness is something frightening: anxiety distorted her kind old face. In vain I explained that though space and a clear view of the earth were missing, I felt like an astronaut with my mask and the effects of the solution, I couldn't convince her that my condition was not serious. Then Valériane came by. I can't have looked too good because she too had a worried face. But she'd thought of bringing along a toothbrush and some Danish toothpaste that tastes of raspberries: my palate and my tongue applauded frenetically; it was a change from the taste of fungus of cortisone.

And while Valériane with all her talent for humour was struggling to lighten the rather thick atmosphere in the room, my brother Vincent arrived. That was so excellent: maybe it was the sunset spreading out beyond the window, but those two turned crimson, and even I felt warm all over.

Like in front of a brazier.

◆

I DREAMT ABOUT it for a week, its long slender silhouette, its outmoded paleness, and the glorious moment when it would slip between my lips, I dreamt its casual and piquant odour that would change abruptly when I set it on fire; I stroked it with my fingertips, rolled it in the palm of my hand, held it against my cheek, touched it lightly with the tip of my tongue, just a little, so it wouldn't get too wet; in advance I savoured its sinful taste— who can boast nowadays of having a sinful taste?— and this desire helped me get better quickly. Oh, they were lasciviously enthralling, those drags on my first cigarette! (I can already hear the anti-smokers complaining: leave me alone, I have every right to smoke here, it's MY book!)

I spent the week holed up in bed, floating feebly in my usual smells: fresh sheets, sandalwood incense, oil of lavender in the perfumer on the bedside table.

Rolled up in a smooth ball within easy reach, Chapter Two waited patiently.

It was exhausting just to watch the buds on the birch tree opening in the alley beyond my window.

I listened to the children yelling with pleasure outside.

The moment had the feel of an old stuffed teddy bear after a nightmare when you're little.

In the morning or the afternoon, Valériane would come by and forcefully administer "The Cadillac." Afterwards her arms were limp, and from having coughed so much, my insides were scraped raw (which I'd rather have done by a car metaphor than by a lover). And for some inexplicable reason, my brother Vincent always managed to arrive five minutes after Valériane, bringing a bowl of steaming hot bouillon, as though he and Valériane arranged to meet at my bedside. But each time they both energetically denied that it was anything but chance. And each time I was thankful that I could be witness to such a charming mystery.

My only form of exercise was to slowly go down the stairs in search of my newspapers on the doorstep. Yesterday morning, a miracle, a real miracle: hidden inside the imposing Wednesday edition of *La Presse* I found *Echine*, the latest novel by Philippe Djian! I didn't think there was a bonus with my subscription, or that I'd won a prize in some competition I participated in; I preferred to think of it as a miracle: illness makes you feel mystical, every feverish person will confirm this.

The miracle-worker identified herself on the phone a few hours later: in the small hours of the morning, as noiseless as a mouse— not really like a mouse though, because Chapter Two didn't move a muscle— my mother had dropped off the surprise. (Most mothers really ought to be sanctified during their lifetimes, which is proof of the flagrant lack of insight on the part of churchmen.)

I should have rationed my little sources of enjoyment, but I couldn't; I read Dijan in fourth gear, even kept him in bed with me at night so I

could touch him in my sleep; I trembled over him
for three days: solitude brings on curious forms of
sensual pleasure.

◆

TODAY IS THE first day I got dressed. I put on a
shrieking scarlet mini-dress just for a change and
decided to go see Violette. It was still fresh out-
side, but the sun was shining; along the way I
stopped at a *Café-Terrasse* on Saint-Denis with a
large bowl of sweet mocha as my only partner;
never did coffee seem more delectable, and the
city cradled me in its waves of gleaming cars,
everything was odorous... it was the day for gar-
bage collection, but even the diverse fumes of
putrescent garbage reassured me, life was sending
me a thousand, ten thousand kisses, I was ready
to forgive everything, everybody, even almost
Crépin Vandégueux, who by now may well be
sensing the caress of spring from the depths of his
coma. Still, I had taken care to put my Opinel
knife into my bag, just in case, a laughable pre-
caution really: you'd have time to rape me ten
times before I could find it in all the clutter I carry

with me, let alone open the blade, but you reassure yourself as best you can. As best you can.

I talked to Violette stretched out on the floor in the bright bands of sunlight by her bed. Through the delicious smoke of her Camels, Violette has only two topics of conversation, at least with me: how to write a funny novel that is both moving and spare, and how to love while being loved, subjects which as we know are multi-faceted, and therefore fascinating. Then her daughters, Mélisse and Gentiane, came back from school with other kids from the neighbourhood, the apartment filled to the brim with jokes and fun spreading out everywhere. Violette sat down at the piano to play a Bach minuet that she punctuated with "Shit!" every time she hit a wrong note, and I went over to the window with my sketch pad and pencil to do a bit of drawing. I like drawing; it makes you notice important details. Suddenly all the kids pressed around me and I had to do a portrait of each one, of Chaillot, seven years old, with a head like a cheerful cherry, of Hansel, ten years old and fragile as the fog, snuggling up close to me. I couldn't stop thinking that I must suddenly have died and landed in paradise, there was such an honest, open happiness, and I breathed it in deeply.

◆

THE WORST THING in the world is that I no longer know. I never really did know, but now it's worse. Much worse. Now I'm really scared. At the time when I was constantly lying, it was bearable, I could keep up a conversation, and make responses, but now when after countless internal reprimands I manage to open my mouth, my actor's voice is nothing but a memory of a distant earlier life. I stutter, and when people ask me to repeat what I said because obviously they didn't grasp it, I gasp and emit the most ridiculous little giggle possible, which makes people think I suffer from congenital idiocy. When I say people, don't misunderstand me, I mean men. Vandégueux did not improve the overall situation: with him, there wasn't a problem at all, the conversation rolled right along without stumbling over even the slightest obstacle. With the result we all know about, I won't insist on it, you understand.

All that dislocates me.

Today when I went out for my daily errands, a cat was meowing somewhere in the street. I listened closely because it was an atrocious noise: something between the screech of a poorly-greased brake and the whine of the electric saw in the frozen meat section at the butcher's. I looked for the cat because I was afraid he might be seriously hurt, and the most graceful tabby emerged from under a doorstep to rub up against my ankles. Nicknaming him (creaky) Hinge, I stooped to scratch his head, and he leapt onto my shoulder with greater elegance than Baryshnikov and stopped meowing, which was a blessing. Both of us purring with happiness, we walked to the corner of the street, then he ran off on urgent business and I asked myself whether maybe my soul had long whiskers if I could cajole a cat so effectively and be so ineffective with guys.

◆

CAN ANYONE TELL me why at certain full moons you can hear the trains bewailing their departures across the sleeping city?

Finally I was asleep, finally, finally... but I was

woken up in the middle of it by (creaky) Hinge
who was screwing like the summer in the alley.
On the bed Chapter Two did a perilous backward
triple jump combined with a salto (worthy of an
Olympic gold medal), then with her belly flat to
the ground she headed for the window. She's a cat
who listens a lot, if not too much. I moved to the
living room at the front of the house, smoked a
cigarette and watched its glow in the blue light of
the moon, and the faraway train pulled me
aboard; I watched the scenery unfold, I took in
the smell of the worn vinyl seats, and behind me
I heard the black porter humming a blues from
the period of the cotton harvests. I was obsessed
by one question: at which exact moment will
Pierre-Marie Moustache let me remove his
glasses?[10]

---

10. I have to give you a chance to understand. Every first
Wednesday of the month, there's a meeting in a bar near me
called Le Mélodie, organized by The Book-Addicts. (Female
addicts are also admitted). They invite one author and interview
him or her for about an hour. I go there to talk to old Monsieur
Tranquille and his youthful memory, but especially because over
the last six months there have been two authentic cases of

thunderstruck love at first sight at Le Mélodie (one involving the interviewer and an evanescent short story writer, and the other between a very promising novelist and a forty-year-old rebellious columnist). Maybe there's a lightning rod hidden in the place somewhere. I don't know. I'll keep warm on the others' love affairs while I wait for the next storm.

So, three weeks ago I was there with this Haitian writer, we're both the same age and in the same type of exile, I'm comfortable with him: he tells brilliant, transparent lies (I won't give you his name, it's fake anyway). I pointed out a new arrival to him, noting his writer's look, both sharp and distracted. The violent shock that the sight of his leonine head and carpenter's hands set off in my soul, I kept secret. The Haitian, who knows the names of numerous deceased and living, told me right away, "That's Pierre-Marie Moustache, a journalist, he's twenty-five." Immediately, my breasts sagged to my waist, and the circles under my eyes drooped to my chin. But I still dragged myself off my chair, pushing away the weightbar of the years, and stepped silently up to Pierre-Marie Moustache.

I didn't have to introduce myself because he knew my books, and accompanied by a young homosexual, beautiful as a legend, and the Haitian, we were soon at a table in L'Européen, a trendy bar not far from Le Mélodie.

I have observed that my invisibility rate reaches a high point

_____

when I like a man, and that is now confounded by my
abysmal inability to speak, but that Wednesday evening it
wasn't too obvious because the three men prattled
continuously till late evening. I laughed when required, and
with each glance he cast in my direction, Pierre-Marie
Moustache looked a little more like a ripening tomato. I
especially remember that at one point, he took his head in
his hands and complained about how difficult it was to have
to spill his guts in order to write.

I found that moving. I could have responded that for me
writing was a voluptuous pleasure, alongside loving and
living, but you're starting to get to know me: I kept still.

So here is an almost infallible recipe for a good strong
fantasy:

— take the humidity of a city (Montreal at the end of June
will do just fine);

— add a night of insomnia, regular or not;

— season generously with the yeowls of two cats swooning
beneath your bedroom window;

— dust with rays of the full moon;

— whip everything up well with the memory of a guy you
met three weeks earlier, who did not completely ignore you;

— simmer in your mind the time it takes to smoke a
cigarette, and voilà!

Now that you have the baggage you need, get on a *Schienenbus* with me between Bad Karlshafen and Ascheberg. Join the convoy of insomnia.

It is a moist summer evening near the solstice, the sun laminating the edge of the horizon. We have to walk single file along the corridor of this train from the nineteen-fifties. Let's look for them in a smoking compartment, one of the emptier ones. There they are, in second class. He's alone, and she's alone. He is facing the direction of the train's movement, and in front of him, with her face turned toward the fields, is my slender self, watching for the occasional villages and their dishevelled gardens. Just now two old men gestured extravagantly at the travellers from the middle of their whimsical rose gardens. She is smoking the Craven A cigarettes she brought from Montreal, he's got the aromatic Peter Stuyvesant. She thinks that with his diaphanous complexion, his excessively blond hair (neatly tied back for the moment) and his oceanic eyes, he is the true aryan type, more so than all the other Germans she's seen among the sixty-year-old railway employees. She wonders how she could get him to take off his glasses, an old-fashioned pair with metal frames, and also when she'll be able to undo his hair. At the far end of the carriage, the black man is endlessly humming the blues. But she also wonders whether one more hurricane wouldn't just smash her soul, forever.

The light is still refusing to die out.

Just in case, she locates a condom in the clutter of her delapidated bag, and hides it in the pocket of her ample dark skirt. Just in case, I swear. She and the pseudo-German observe each other surreptitiously, and rather than turn on the ghastly neon lights above their heads, he uses a flashlight to read through a sheaf of loose pages, in which he corrects a word from time to time. Maybe it's a manuscript, if she's lucky it's a manuscript. Just about every quarter of an hour, the train stops at a station and the doors open automatically: from the platform you hear, "Gute Nacht, Albrecht!", and Albrecht, doubtless the conductor, invariably replies, "Glauben Sie, es wird sich aufklären?", before he blasts a strident note on his whistle, the doors close and the journey continues. Toward which real or internal borders?

No one ever gets on. She thinks vaguely that the monotonous movement is hypnotizing her, dissolving all her resistances. But look, look! She's setting her right foot between the stranger's feet, deliberately, I'm sure! He smiles at her, she puts a finger to her lips, what would be the use of talking since they probably wouldn't understand each other? Then he turns off his flashlight and puts it down next to the notebook. He takes her foot, unlaces the worn Derby, slips off her soiled sock, and laughs quietly as he sees the navy blue polish on her toenails. Slowly, with infinite patience, he massages her metacarpi, the ball of her foot, her instep, her ankle, the Achilles tendon. Every now and then he raises his head and smiles at her. She has the impression that her right foot is becoming the supple and powerful paw of a panther, and her left foot is completely shrivelled, sickly. That's where all the sadness of her childhood is collected, the period when she wore the execrably heavy corrective shoes that were so cumbersome and prevented her skipping and bouncing around like the other little girls. She would like the stranger to know all this, her absolutely urgent need for tenderness and her fear of breaking at the slightest shock, but she doesn't say anything because now he is massaging her left foot as though he understood all her former un-happiness. "Gute Nacht, Albrecht!", a strident whistle, the doors, which borders?

But look, look! He's brought her left foot up to his mouth, he's covering it with fluid kisses, he's delicately sucking on a toe and playing his tongue around it, the air is growing heavy with a sea of intoxicating smells, a wave of pleasure sets her aglow to the hairline, she goes soft as a caramel, she stops herself moaning. She watches him through half-closed eyes, vibrating in the length-ening moment, languishing. Now she's setting her right foot into the man's crotch, at the base of the strong turgescence whose flaming call she can feel through the cloth. The young man has let go her other foot, he slides forward to give her caress more room, and now he's the one who tips back his head and closes his eyes while she indolently deepens his desire.

But they hear the nonchalant refrain of Albrecht's voice drawing near, "Fahrkarten, bitte. Fahrkarten, bitte... Danke schön." With the same movement, they sit up, present their tickets, look out the window, surprised that the night has already absorbed the countryside.

After checking their tickets, Albrecht hesitates a moment before going, with perhaps a tinge of complicity below his moustache. They are looking at each other, but now a certain ill temper hovers between them. She takes her bag and goes out into the corridor. She lowers the window and despite the trilingual sign forbidding her to do so, leans out into the wind. The man joins her, lights up two cigarettes, hands her one and leans out too, nudged up close against her. Excited, she breathes in his light blond sweat, and muses about another, more concealed, fleshly fragrance. In spite of the late hour, he doesn't have any beard stubble, so she could spend hours kissing him and not abrade her face. The doors open again, "Glauben Sie es wird sich aufklären?", which borders? The blues unroll lazily within her, far off, the hills have grown round, her cigarette end streaks the darkness with an ephemeral arabesque. She studies the stranger's thoughtful profile, the mouth that has never been ravaged by bitterness. He turns toward her. In slow motion, she raises her hands to the back of his neck. To undo his light hair. Loosen it up. She almost faints. They stay like that. Motionless. Petrified.

Two comets are about to merge.

Lust grips her soul. She goes to the end of the carriage, enters the washroom but doesn't lock the door. What do all the little sorrows matter when hope is rushing through her veins?

She leans on the edge of the chilly sink; she's taken off her panties and stuffed them into the other pocket of her ample dark skirt. The train is devouring its track. Occasionally, the light of a streetlamp makes a gash in the dark. If the man doesn't arrive soon, she thinks her heart will burst out of her chest and escape.

But here he is, pushing open the door of the narrow cubicle and closing it behind him. They are face to face, at the edges of a fever. So vulnerable. So eager that the whole train seems to be in flames with them. The man holds the door shut with one hand behind him, if he locks it the neon will come on. But he doesn't move. He waits for the woman to make a first move toward him. She takes off his glasses, balances them on the soap dispenser. Then the man tugs her close with his free arm. As though neither he nor she could ever still their hunger, their thirst, the kiss draws on, violent and merciless. Their mouths, their teeth, their tongues, like wild beasts, like fleshy crevices.

She pulls away from him. To stir him even more she slowly undoes the buttons of his shirt. Then she takes off her sweater with the fluid grace of a torero. She rubs her nipples against the man's chest, and the kiss reconnects them, submerges them, besplatters their ears, their throats, their shoulders, while their loins are getting ready, growing eager, crying out.

Then the man lets go of the doorknob, lays her one foot against his neck, plants the other against the door. He kneels down between her thighs, raises her ample skirt to her waist. He nips at her slender hip, touches her navel, runs his teeth through the dark curls, sips the moist beads at the base of her groin, then with his fingers he traces the edges of the outer lips, spreads wide the inner ones, and grasps the sacred pod, vibrating his tongue, and she, sucked up by her pleasure, grasps the man's hair in order not to fly away.

He's getting up, hugging her to him, smiling, then he reaches into his trouser pocket. Still breathless, she takes the packet from her skirt pocket and opens her hand for him. His smile grows wider and he shows her a similar packet;

as a game he takes hers, hides them behind his back and then shows her his two closed fists so she can choose. She touches his left hand, he opens it, his is the winner. He leans toward her, feels for her skirt pocket, puts the extra condom back in, and takes advantage of the moment to devastate her throat once more. Click, clack, she undoes his belt buckle, he undresses in one move and a slash of light blinds her view of the shaft reaching for her Eden. With a hot prayer, she enlaces her fingers in his to roll the film down over the incandescent totem, she can't help touching behind the silken bag, playing with the living jewels, but impatience is ravishing her, she moves forward, an open fruit toward the brandished penis, and with infinite slowness the man finally plunges into her. Their rhythms adapt, flourish, grip one another, reel, veer, hurl, flow; and the *Schienenbus* enters an interminable tunnel joined by another deafening turbo-train from the other direction, muffling the raucous noise of their pleasure. Which border? which borders?

Afterwards, afterwards, they are still entangled, they have waited for their hearts and their breathing to grow calm, for their sex to glow down. He strokes her cheek, she touches his hair one last time, before they readjust their clothing. With a secret smile they emerge into the deserted corridor, and collapse in each others arms on the worn vinyl seat.

She sleeps as well as if she were in a bed at the "Georges V" in Paris, had received the Prix Goncourt two days earlier and had been interviewed on *Apostrophe* the day before.

In the morning he is gone. He has left her a pack of Peter Stuyvesant's. Albrecht has also got off during the night. It is misty, and cooler. Her first thought is for the numerous children she saw during her stay, babies with horribly burnt sweet little faces and hands. In particular, she thinks about the mother she ended up asking in her hesitant German, who shrugged her shoulders in absolute distress and finally responded with just one word: Chernobyl.

How can she, how can I still dream in this century of nightmares?

"Glauben Sie es wird sich aufklären?": do you think the sky will clear?

◆

ALL RIGHT, ALL RIGHT, all right. Let's calm down. Hello reality.

Otherwise you won't see the summer pouring in, and I won't either. Still, you could say that its megatons of tropical humidity have already filled Montreal to overflowing, though we're far away from the sea— unfortunately. Right downtown the cicadas (which I think must be mythical) are chirring louder than the traffic— honestly! I don't know what to wear any more, in less than an hour even the lightest fabric is heavy with sweat, I can't write completely naked, can I? (I'm already very naked when I write) so I've resigned myself to wearing the same oversize and worn T-shirt every day, the one with a Picasso print on it, easily reassuring myself: "Good old Pablo would have worked even in a furnace." I sprayed the last drops of my perfume into a Chinese fan, and when I can't stand it any more I fan between my legs. I think I must be downright crazy: honestly, writing stories like the one in the last chapter, during the worst of the dog days, growing moist with ink when I'm already dripping wet everywhere else!...

(Poor crazy lady: lock me up tight somewhere, put me into a strait jacket to stop me masturbating, and above all, fill me up with psychotropic drugs to break down my obsessions, set me free, help, set me free!)

But on the other hand, I'm thankful that literature lets me lie down with her, a book makes up for not having a beach, and a man of letters is better than none.

Chapter Two has been perfecting her imitation of a rug; she looks like a hunting trophy of the greenhouse effect, she spreadeagles so wide on the floor that I've had to watch to make sure she's still breathing.

I went out for my usual walk, with my feet in the ethereal ecstasy of my sandals. Since my mother, Marguerite, thinks there is nothing more vulgar than a woman who smokes on the street, I always light a cigarette to her health; that way I'm in complete harmony with the steaming asphalt, and so is she. I stick my nose into every florist's display, into every decorative flowerpot installed by the local council, and I get high on pollen (it's a lot less expensive and so much more effective than a beer). And seeing that because of my move

I can now walk down to Les Atriums, I make every use of it, for the AIR CONDITIONING. The albino goldfish isn't there any more. Nor are the two young tramps. Maybe they ate the fish. Or the other way round. I don't know. You only see really old tramps there now. Dressed up warm as though it were always winter for them.

So how far have I got with my characters? Here's the news: my neighbour Valériane and my brother Vincent are coming right along. He says about her: "She's the firefly in my darkroom." And she says about him: "I don't need the sea, I swim in the blue of his eyes." I have supper with them sometimes, and we'll be in the middle of a conversation when suddenly their eyes hook each other and poof! the universe around them, including my own little self, fades away. They are the sugar in the city's *grand café*.

One wind-still lunchtime when she was hanging out her sheets on the clothesline, I also saw Dahlia again, Valériane's sister, who just came back from a triumphant tour of Europe. She'd just left her lover and whispered "What can you do, you have to wash away gardens from the past." Poor thing, her tears evaporated as they fell.

One steamy evening Pierre-Pierre invited me to dinner on a Saint-Denis terrace. Contrary to all the dictates of basic common sense he was wearing an impeccable long-sleeved sand-coloured shirt, a spotless pair of earth-coloured trousers, a pair of brand new Italian shoes and ochre socks: I was in a sweat for him. He tried to seduce me, but as night fell the twilight of loss took hold. What do you want Pierre-Pierre, I can't go back: between you and me there's a little corpse less than three centimeters long that didn't even have the chance to be given a name. Its memory rests too heavily in my belly for me to dally with you.

Another day, Mélisse and Gentiane, Violette's daughters, stole my fountain pen and my notebook for just a moment, to write me a *billet-doux* beneath a purple ink sketch of palm trees; you can't complain about solitude when you carry something like that around with you, right next to the Opinel knife in your worn old bag.

To prove that the globe is no larger than a black dot, and there's no reason to be pretentious or proud, and we're just infinitesimally small fragments yearning in vain for happiness, it has just turned out that Valériane, who works in film, was hired for the same team as Pierre-Marie Moustache's wife, Angélique. One Sunday afternoon when I was floating like a wisp of smoke high in the implacable sky, at about twenty thousand meters, and everything below me looked like a child's game, I happened to meet her briefly at Valériane's. To summarize: Angélique Moustache radiates a beauty that sparkles with health, a smooth skin, ten years younger than me, and the kind of confidence that reciprocal love inspires. I'm not lying when I say that with a single blow gravity reassumed its despicable rights over me, and my soul was crushed like a *crêpe bretonne* on the cement, no parachute or anything else. Hello reality.

This goddamn imbecilic heart of mine, rushing around, too hard, too fast, wanting too much to be in love, quaking at the slightest glance! If I could just drag it out of my chest, cut it into thin slices, fry it up and make a good meal of it, this damn imbecilic heart!!! And quite honestly, how in the world can I be preoccupied with all this while in Burundi (a country the size of a thumbnail in my atlas), twenty-five thousand people have just been killed in the course of a single week? A real massacre, downright genocide: the Tutsis armed with machine guns and in helicopters, against the Mutus, mainly peasants; I don't know anything about the circumstances of the incident because information about Africa is hard to get, not even one column on the back page of *La Presse*, and no more than twenty seconds on *Radio Canada*, so I have to invent everything, especially the worst of it: dismembered five-year-olds, crowds of refugees, disoriented in the painful nights scarred by mortars, you can see I'm still letting myself be swept along by the images, from just reading the line "twenty-five thousand killed in one week," like a bloody gash across the morning paper. I ask you the question, but I already know the answer: it's because I'm sheltered, absolutely safe, here with you in these pages, and in real life, where everything terrifies me, starting with the toxic cloud of biphenal polychloride dioxins and furans from the fire at Saint-Basile-le-Grand... and why stop there, I'm just as horrified by Reagan, Ceaucescu, Khomeini, and all the other obnoxious specimens who are just as lost in their rambles as I am; so, why not just write it all: in the smallest possible frame, I no longer have the courage to live, period. Somewhere between the effervescently wild imaginings and the dreadful cruelty of reality, you can understand my choice. You have to keep on living though, so I hope you'll excuse me, but I won't be coming back here until I've at least tried; I don't know how much time will have gone by when you turn the page, a month, a year, ten years, but I swear that I want to, and will attempt the impossible: engage in my last, and only tangible struggle, to live in the present, for real, before I die.

◆

(I'M NOT BACK for good; I just want to say this: I think that somewhere at the bottom of a wound I must have lost the directions for living. But which wound? I haven't got time to look. I'm trying to invent a new way of existing. See you later.)

◆

(THINGS DON'T MOVE by themselves for me; the "here" is all right, it's the "now" that's out of reach, while the conditional and the elsewhere want to keep me confined. More later.)

◆

(YESTERDAY EVENING I went to the theatre with Violette to see Robert Lepage's *Trilogy of the Dragons*, a truly restless piece. During the second intermission she asked me how I would like to die if I had the choice. At the age of ninety-nine, I replied, during a party with champagne and helium-filled balloons, surrounded by all my women friends, my fifteen children and twenty-three grandchildren... if I had the choice. And my left hand raised, my last words would be, "Hey! Taxi!" As for Violette, she'd rather die quickly, in the dark, and alone. She added, "The one time I did die, it was just like that, I was on the ground, behind a closed door, there was no bed, not even a mattress, nothing. It's no longer my death that scares me. There's no need to panic about dying. I would even say it relieves you of a big burden." I agreed, as you can imagine. Life is what requires incommensurably more talent. And life is a novel, as everyone knows except me.)

◆

(I AM A HAUNTED house that has generated its own ghosts who are now pitilessly suffocating me. I think about Pierre-Marie Moustache and all the layers of dreams I adorned him with; and I tell myself that's the exact reason why I don't get anywhere: when I'm face to face with him, the myth I have created squashes the trembling ant I have become under its enormous boot; while if I hadn't dreamt about him, communication would be possible, honest, down to earth. Less distressing, you might say. I should listen to you more often.

So, the program of the day, the hour, the moment: hello reality, I'm afraid of you, but I'm diving in, trying not to hold my breath. Could you be just a little gentle?)

It's gray outside.

It's gray inside.

◆

TODAY I GOT ON the number 80 bus; it's a line I like because it's used by every nationality. Just by ear

I could have taken a lightning trip from Port-au-Prince to Tokyo with a detour via Santiago, Chile, but I controlled myself; this intifada for sovereignty of the moment is trying. There was a smell of star anise, plantain and water of orange blossom. No one can forbid the joy of scents.

Then I saw one of the last wasps of autumn beating itself against the window. We were riding in one of the new buses whose designers I definitely cannot congratulate, only the top parts of the louvered windows open, and toward the inside, which is quite absurd because you boil in the summer and freeze in the winter. I caught the wasp carefully by the wings and after I fumbled around with the other hand to undo the catch, I tossed it out. I know this little gesture won't help anyone in Biafra. But it's better than nothing. At least I think so.

In this state of mind I returned to my good old rue Saint-Denis, to Le Braque, where I ordered a coffee dusted with chocolate (the doctors have forbidden me to have chocolate because of an old case of mastitis, but they didn't forbid me to drink it, ha, ha...). Death is really too near to deprive myself. To describe the atmosphere just a little more clearly: when I sprinkled the three packs of sugar over the top of my coffee to make it even sweeter, the granules formed a heart-shape on the frothy milk. By accident, I swear. I took care not to destroy it with a sudden stir of my spoon. The heart ended up going under because of its weight.

I felt I was in a timeless hole, as though nothing had moved here since I was fifteen. In one corner one of the regulars was sipping his orangeade, a little further back a student was cramming through her inevitable stack of notes, and an over-dressed couple, real estate agents maybe, were ending what seemed to be a secret rendez-vous. They were holding hands, whispering sweet nothings of the penny-candy variety, which made the rest of us invisible.

That's when he came in. Heh! he was impossible to miss in his suit of quilted cotton that was rather large on him, bagged out and spotted with countless stains. He moved in jerks, with one leg shooting off in one direction and the other leg going the opposite way; his head shook in spasms and his arms gesticulated wildly. I couldn't help thinking of a marionette with an invisible and sadistic operator (if I weren't already an atheist I would have become one right there). Stuttering horribly, he asked if he could sit at my table. I said yes. With formidable will power, he grasped hold of the chair that was a lot less wobbly than he was, and after several unsuccessful attempts, finally stabilized himself on its seat. The waitress, a full-bosomed dyed-redhead, brought him a coffee. It couldn't have been the first time she served him, the cream was already in the coffee, there was no spoon, and she put a large stack of paper napkins beside him. After a few missed passes, the spastic was able to grab hold of his cup with two hands and bring it to his mouth. But on the way, half of the coffee spilt over his sweater. He grinned and said spastics wouldn't be quite as skinny if their stomachs were located outside their bodies and their clothing, but still below the heart, just like for everyone else.[11] I laughed too, till I was in tears, and said yes, that's for sure.

It's a good thing time was standing still at Le Braque, because I would have grown visibly older

---

11. I'm summarizing here. If I were to transcribe everything faithfully, it would be virtually endless, and I have to save paper; I'm low on cash.

we spent so long talking. He told me about every-
thing, his little life, his little Asocial Assistance
cheque, his little room, his soda biscuits, his soda
biscuit crumbs, his little transistor, his little sav-
ings that two or three times a year paid for a
prostitute, always the same one who would fuck
him on condition he wore a paper bag over his
head.

He seemed so full, and I so empty. But he'd
never experienced love, and I had... I can't lie
about that. I caught hold of his gesticulating
hands, held them down on the table, and said, "If
you like, I'll tell you a story and masturbate you
at the same time, below the tablecloth. What do
you say?" His head wagged like the clanger in a
bell, but since his hands stayed on the edge of the
table and his eyes filled with lovely spring water,
I gathered he said yes. I pulled my chair up to his.
I took off my right shoe, and for safety's sake put
my foot on his left one, to stop him from kicking.
Then I leaned my cheek into my left hand, slipped
the other hand under the tablecloth, grasped hold
of him, he already had a skyscraper erection, and
said,

"Let's imagine that the world is different. I

would be rich, and so would you. Today we'd be in Paris, in the first arrondissement, it would still be warm, but I would be wearing my marvellous white fox coat..."

(Heh, he's not wearing underwear; understandable, it must take him ages just to put on his sweater and pants in the morning; why bother with such futilities?)

"... I'd be imitating one of Baudelaire's characters, naked under my coat, covered in all my gold filigree, my ornaments, I'd be a real walking fortune, with all the diamond bracelets, silver and ruby necklaces, I would have put on too much jewellery and it would tinkle and chime joyously. Underneath, I'd be naked, except for my legs sheathed in garterless stockings, Dior stockings at fifty dollars a pair, black ones with a strass rose at the ankle, and expensive shoes, flats inlaid with real cobra. I wouldn't have any second thoughts about the foxes, the snakes or the black miners in South Africa; since I would be rich, I'd have forgotten all my ecological and humanitarian principles...

(I'm in no hurry, my hand slowly goes up and down his penis, I play with his testicles, because my story is only just beginning.)

"... still, the stockings will leave a mark at the top of my thighs, when I take them off in a little while, there'll be a big V on my skin, like a pink arrow pointing toward my sex. I'd go to the Café Costes, packed as usual and still just as ugly with its steel furniture. I wouldn't wait around, but go straight down to the washrooms in the basement. Just like the day before, I would have greased the palm of the toilet-lady with a thousand franc note, and her withered fingers decorated with costume jewellery rings would make a conniving little gesture. She'd whisper, 'He's already there,' meaning you...

(I accelerate the movement now, encircle the foreskin as I move up and down. The man emits a kind of gurgling which must be a moan of pleasure, at least I assume so, since he doesn't try to pull away from my caress.)

"... I'd go into the ladies' washroom, the most elegant in the world with its fixtures like sculptured cascades, and as we'd agreed, I'd knock twice and then three times on the door of the second cabin of mirrors. From inside you would turn the handle, or rather the sphere serving as a handle, and I would enter. You would be there, dressed like an English prince in a Montana suit, a hopeful green, I would kiss you forever, as though we had all the time in the world, as though there were neither bombs nor pollution crushing us under their mortal threat. You would undo my coat and your hands would fly over the sky of my skin like kites alarmed by the sirocco. Then I'd help you undress, you'd sit down on the bowl, and one after the other I'd take off my stockings, with the lascivious gestures of the most vulgar stripper. You would parody the French and say, "Please don't forget to put your pumps back on!", which would make me die laughing, and you'd laugh with me, in a way you never laughed before. And our laughter would be infinitely multiplied in the triangle of mirrors around us. You would be naked; with my one stocking I would tie your feet down to the starboard and port sides of the bowl, with the other I would bind your hands behind you to stop you from wriggling. And then, still in my furs, I would straddle you..."

(That's when he exploded, throwing himself across the table with a loud cry. No one in Le Braque flinched, he was probably a client known

for his tricks, his yells, and his unhappiness. I
stroked his hair, gave him a light kiss goodbye,
and went home. Outside, the night breeze was
whistling lightly for once.)

◆

WINTER'S COMING ON, the bastard's early this year.
And like all those single parents or unemployed
people under thirty without unemployment in-
surance, in a word, the poor of this country, I
don't heat my place. Not yet. Not right away. I
endure. I write in leather gloves with the fingers
cut off, Chapter Two warms my feet as best she
can, I write, I write in order to forget that I'm
shivering. I imagine that I'm in the Sargasso Sea,
the sun's toes are dallying with the absinthe green
waves, I only have to open my jaws for some
exquisite plankton to slip by my plate of baleen
and fill my belly, I'm warbling, almost in tune with
another whale, a male, as happy as I am to be
letting his tail and his fins slide past debonnaire
sea urchins and myriads of shimmering little fish,
too numerous for each to have its own name. And
I imagine I have the right to avoid shivering while

I write. But when the cold gets unbearable, I escape from my refrigerator and take refuge at the 2323, a bar nearby. Muscade, the young waitress, is very understanding; there's no problem if I take two or three hours to sip my coffee. As night comes crashing down, idiotically earlier every day, I go hide away under my electric blanket turned on high; that way only the tip of my nose freezes. Welcome to my dazzling social life!

◆

YESTERDAY I CARRIED OUT a tiny little act of courage, which, I admit, did have to do with my personal survival. Courage is a muscle like all the others: you have to exercise it from time to time to maintain it. So this is what happened: for years my doctors have been harping on about the fact that there's nothing more harmful for my asthma than cat fur. It's true, I can feel it now that the windows are as good as condemned for the winter. So, holding back my tears, I took my affectionate and understanding little Chapter Two, placed her in a container with an opening she could breathe through, took the subway at

Sherbrooke, and sixteen stations later (a modern Way of the Cross) I arrived at Namur station and the Canadian Society for the Prevention of Cruelty to Animals to give my kitty up for adoption or to sure death. Poor thing, she was still purring in my arms when the employee took her from me, but her heart was pounding. And I was able to prevent myself crying because, honestly, there are things much more painful than losing a pet: with the world situation growing worse, you have to maintain at least a grain of stoicism, what the hell. What the hell.

To avoid going back to an empty home and the phantom of a cat, I went to Le Mélodie, where a guy involved me in a discussion. He was a rather drunken imbecile, deliberately abrasive. He gave me a tedious lecture, about how when a man and a woman are together and the woman gets pregnant and doesn't want to keep the baby, but the man wants it, then the mother should have the baby anyway, give birth to it, and hand it over to the father after. The guy kept on about his sperm being valuable, and about his struggle to defend the rights of sperm. I tried to argue that sperm certainly did have some importance, but that the blood, the belly and the heart of the woman were equally important, but I got nowhere, he trotted out all kinds of intellectual arguments that had no connection with life, claiming among other idiocies that pregnancy was a primitive and natural condition, and that feminists had complicated everything.

I left him sitting there, not without hating myself for wasting a really sludgy hour with that creep. In spite of the psychological suffering linked to the operation, I'd unconditionally approve of any woman who aborted that particular gent. What depresses me most are the people who have urine where their brains should be, and shit instead of hearts.

So when I got back home, I phoned the government to offer my services as a foster home for a child. If I can lighten the life of someone under twelve, I don't see why I should hold back. Stupidity is too stifling and death too near for me to deprive myself.

◆

I TOLD MARGUERITE, my mother, about my decision. The only fault you can find with this woman, who is so generous, is that she says no to certain aspects of life, at least of my life. "You're too fragile, too fragile!" she said in alarm. She was sobbing as though I had a terminal form of cancer. Hold on, Marguerite, it may be true that I was born with a soul like a brook, but let's not exaggerate, I've survived a good many disasters, nonetheless! My mother's attitude made me really unhappy, but then I didn't worry about it too much, she won't be able to stop herself loving the child when she sees her. As for Violette, she was much more enthusiastic, "At least you won't get allergies from a child, it doesn't have any fur." Good old Violette; always good for a laugh.

◆

SHE'D FORGOTTEN HIM. Didn't think about it any more. It was about three years ago, in the middle of the coldest winter. They'd met in a café. They'd discussed literature passionately, but said so little about their lives. At his place later that night, on a mattress on the floor, he'd revealed the countenance of his joy, the solemn fury of orgasm. But he'd kept his eyes closed. She'd forgotten him. Didn't think about it any more. Two days later she flew to Paris, to her sister's, and from there she wrote him a letter each word of which plucked at her heartstrings. He hadn't replied. She'd forgotten him. Didn't think about it any more.

It was about three years ago, in the February freeze. Since then, a bit of this and a bit of that, friendships woven and torn, fireflies of desire lighting the eyes, sudden swelling sobs, time silently whitening a hair or two, a woman's days and nights, a woman's fears, a woman's victories, she'd forgotten him. Didn't think about it any more. But yesterday, yesterday in the dying December light, she saw him again. With his mohair voice he untangled the web of her past. Told her about his latest break-up, still moist. Sang her one of his compositions. A song that shattered her, and her already wavering inner self. She'd forgotten, didn't think about it any more. And then his arms around her, a refuge, again and again the incandescent kisses, the amnesia of skin growing iridescent, she'd forgotten, didn't think about it any more.

And when she watches him sleep at night, so calm, so appeased, she remembers the face of another man, a man before this one, still more peaceful. It was before the years of combat in her twenties, before her solidarity with other feminists, before the years of travel and discussion in every corner of Quebec. Before this before, when she was seventeen and in love for the first time, and cut to ribbons by the scissors of life for the first time: she was so studious she'd decided not to drive out of town with him to go to the theatre, she'd decided against the trip with him; then his Volkswagen skidded off the road in the autumn wind, caught against a tree, an impossible bird of pain and death, she'd forgotten, didn't think about it any more. Only the moments of happiness that memory clings to remained like the bright coloured scraps of a worn-out quilt. She'd forgotten, didn't think about it any more. She only remembered the nuances of his eyes, an ultramarine scar, and the disturbance in her soul, dissipating melancholy. Was this metamorphosis into a lake a sign of growing old?

And why does she get stranded in that other gaze full of mist and laughter, the gaze of an eight-year-old boy, her very first love? She can only recall his first name, Jean, and the nickname she gave him, Radium, a new word she'd just learned along with the noun, radiation. And wasn't that exactly what she felt when he waited for her at the street corner under the maple tree? Jean Radium, wreathed in emerald seeds, the maple keys all the other children called helicopters, but whose real name she'd whispered in his ear, "They're samaras, samaras, don't forget," like the tenderest secret, the surest oath. She'd forgotten, she no longer thought about the folded notes that Jean slipped her under the rather long nose of Mademoiselle Gaudreau, the teacher in charge of 3B. She'd created a whole imaginary zoo of antelopes and dinosaurs, parrots and whales, for which Radium kept rigorous track of births and deaths, she'd forgotten, she no longer thought that purity could be woven from this century's violence.

And why Jean, why this name that drifts toward her in the night, perhaps because she's very old now, she's lost her real teeth, and her weakened eyesight shows her the city like a blurred painting, an ineffable and vibrant Pissarro. It is summer in Montreal: it's so hot you can't hear yourself think. If only you could not hear yourself forget. She only takes very small steps now. She sits on the veranda with her companion in old age. They sip real lemonade. Then they play a game that is rather ridiculous, a game reserved for the two of them: he offers her an invisible cigarette, lights it for her with a non-existent lighter, and she smokes a delicious absence. Sometimes, she forgets his name for a moment, words themselves escape her, she no longer thinks about it, and calls her old companion Ocean. And with infinite tenderness he replies, "It's Homer, my sweet, my name is Homer." And sometimes the night still sways in their slow caresses, sometimes their worn skin still glows with joy. And at dawn, sometimes anxiety still lacerates her, she forgets, she forgets, she can't think any more, and then he takes his only healing recipe from the drawer, the only elixir he has for her, and reads her a page or two of her faithful journal. And in the light about them, the quavering voice smooths out all the pain, all the forgetting.

◆

I'M SORRY. Let me rub my face in the dust at your feet. Forgive me. Let me take off your shoes, and bathe your ankles in my tears of contrition (unfortunately my hair is too short to dry them too). Excuse me: I have not only been making things up, I've been telling outright lies from the second half of page 100. I got carried away. Try to understand, I beg you: life is such a bitch, and the page is so serene, so virgin... Try to grasp the power of this lie: on the one hand there's a desert as far as the future stretches, on the other, there's a skinny little woman with all the words at her fingertips, like so many gardens just asking to give off their perfume. In her position, in mine, could you resist? Could you resist the attraction of this gap? You could? Let me congratulate you on your moral rectitude, and ask you to pardon my weakness.

So here's the truth: I met the man about two years ago (I put three years, it's more poignant). And I didn't forget about him either, I even thought about him a lot, sheer masochism, probably. And yesterday he had me listen to fifteen of his songs, not one. Finally, I have to admit that we didn't make love yesterday evening. My heart was all out of shape because it had been a year and one day since anyone put his arms around me, since exactly the morning that my pregnancy test turned dark blue, (if it gets any more positive, you die). And then, yesterday evening, it was more than a week since I had really slept, because that man woke me up from the depths of two years of silence, and invited me to supper at his place: I was loaded down with hopes.

He's a pianist who plays in a chic bar at night, a bar too chic for my poverty; he'd also just spent twenty-five hours at the piano two days earlier for a spontaneous mass rally drive in the *Centre Paul-Sauvé*, and was deathly pale from fatigue. But he still carried me from the kitchen to the bed, and caressed me; he was on his knees at my side, playing both hands across my body, a living synthesizer, and I came with a cry, I'm always ready to burst into orgasm, overflow (a year and a day of chastity will change any body into a pressure cooker); but when I snuggled my nose into the side of his throat, and each cell in my cheek revelled in feeling each whisker in his gently scratchy beard, he suddenly fell asleep. I watched him sleep a good part of the night, still dressed; I undid his runners, pulled the covers over him, put out the lights and watched him snore in the green and red glow from the diodes of his sound system. He didn't have a pillow; I watched him take my sweater, roll it up into a ball and push it under his head, all without opening his eyes. Around three in the morning, I heard a 747 take off, for Africa, I think. Or maybe Armenia, with food and winter clothes for the earthquake survivors, I hope. I watched him snore, and promised myself that in the morning I'd wake him with the best fellatio of his entire life, so extravagant he'd think he was still dreaming. But in the morning I was so sound asleep, he was able to jump out of bed, make me a *café au lait* the way I like, with lots of sugar, and bring it in on a tray before I even began to emerge from my coma. And then I didn't have the courage and I went home cursing my lack of daring.

There. He'll never call me back. Probably. Fortunately there are always rose gardens you can invent, because life itself...

Will my heart always be ashamed, in shreds, and my soul silenced, when I'm with them?

◆

I HATE WINTER even more because of Christmas.
On December 24, at dawn, a tramp died of cold
on a cement bench in Parc Viger. That lends a
curious taste to the *canapés* of *foie gras*, to the
onion soup *au gratin*, to the minced pork *pâté*, to
the stuffed turkey, the mushroom gravy, the fancy
grade green peas, the mashed potatoes with their
crater of sauce, the camembert, the brie and the
cheddar, the three-lettuce salad, the *brioches*, the
cookies, the macaroons, the date squares, the
sorbet, the Christmas *bûche*, though they were all
lovingly prepared by Marguerite, my mother. A
very disagreeable taste. A bitter taste.

It was because of the tramp that I decided to
take my patient some flowers. He can't have had
any visits over the holidays, and on New Year's
Eve it's not very tempting to go look at someone
who is half-dead. I bought a crimson bouquet of
flowers at La Sylve, next door to 2323. The florist
is a comely, pleasant woman, a walking botanic
encyclopedia. I selected an aromatic sprig of Irish
bells, the only spot of greenery, then some car-
mine broom, some rosy freesias, two rubrum

lilies, and as a contrast, one "paper-white" narcissus. Smelling this bouquet with my two feet buried in a snowdrift and waiting for a bus on a night when even party-goers were scarce allowed me to let some of the over-consumption of the hectic period slip into forgetfulness. That's when, suddenly, a total electrical breakdown took out the traffic lights, the opalescent streetlights, the hundreds of multi-coloured decorations on the Portuguese homes, and even the square eyelids of the windows. Suddenly, high above Montreal, all the constellations in the sky opened their majestic arms to me, and I thanked Hydro-Québec for this icy gift.

As usual, the hospital smelled of disinfectant and loneliness. Due to the breakdown, the emergency generators were wreathing the inner corridors in slime-yellow light, and the nurses at the central station were afloat in the aquarium light of their computer screens. Elsewhere, evanescent figures in colourless jackets occasionally wafted through the dimness.

I reached his room without hindrance, invisible as I am. It wasn't a room, just a large windowless closet, with two walls of glassed-in cupboards.

Luckily I have a storm-lighter which I hadn't
forgotten to fill up, because it was dark as the
Vogul's language in there. I put away my lighter,
leaving the door half open so a stream of luminous
slaver flowed into the cupboard. I took off my
woollen hat, my scarf, my gloves and my coat, put
the flowers in the bedpan, and the bouquet of fire
gave off all its perfumes at full blast: oh polyphony
of summer.

I sat down on the edge of the bed. My invalid
seemed smaller lying down than upright, and less
terrifying on his back than on me. His hair was
longer, and so were his nails. His chest rose and
fell; the droplets of solution trickled into his arm;
at that moment his life was the opposite of his
novel: minimalist. A coma's an odd thing: it's not
really sleep, but another dimension, a continent
of peace, a state I was almost envious of; when he
suddenly sneezed, I froze. I thought he was going
to wake up, I didn't know whether to run away or
stay. His lower jaw hung loose, he emitted two or
three death rattles, then stopped breathing. Com-
pletely. I started counting in my head (as I'd
learned in my adolescent first aid courses): one
thousand and one, one thousand and two, up to

one thousand and thirty, and he still hadn't started up again!

I rushed out into the corridor, there was NO ONE at the nurses' station! No nurse, no doctor, no intern, no cat (obviously), NO ONE! At one thousand and forty-six I assessed the situation as follows: if I don't do something, his brain will darken forever in exactly six thousand seconds, maybe I can save him; but then if some day he comes out of his coma, his memory will be intact, and he'll remember that I'm the one who put him here in the first place, and he may want to kill me to take revenge; but why the hell bother with this pointless reasoning, do I make a move or don't I? damn it all, anyway!

At one thousand and forty-seven I leaned over him for mouth to mouth. I had the horrible impression of kissing a cadaver: eight months of coma don't improve a man's breath.

At one thousand one hundred and sixty-three, there were no results, the air wouldn't pass through. I only had till one thousand plus five thousand nine hundred and ninety-nine to save him. Otherwise his heart would stop. No more blood to the brain. Never any more light in his intelligence.

I frantically searched through the cupboards, and in the sixth one I located a plastic pot with a rigid tube in the end. One thousand two hundred and forty-eight, I pulled off the plastic tube.

At one thousand two hundred and eighty-one I lit my storm-lighter at the first attempt (it understood the urgency of the situation) and with the flame, I disinfected the blade of the Opinel knife that I'd carried around in my bag since the attempted rape.

At one thousand two hundred and ninety-five, in order to have better light, I had my lighter propped against a metal plate that leaned against the forehead of the almost-deceased.

One thousand three hundred and seven, I touched the throat of the clinically dead patient just below the Adam's apple and got my bearings.

One thousand three hundred and eight, I took a deep breath to gather courage, and holding his skin between thumb and forefinger, I cut Crépin Vandégueux's throat. Not very much really: I sliced open the epidermis, a cut almost seven centimeters long. It bled pretty heavily.

I saw the trachea, fluted, whitish, and round; at one thousand three hundred and twenty-five I'd cut into the soft part between two rings; at one thousand three hundred and twenty-seven I tried to slip the plastic tube into the trachea, which was difficult because of its viscosity and the glands round about, too near, that were getting in the way. Death encircled my wrists with its icy phalanges. Quick! Quick!

At one thousand three hundred and thirty-nine, the tube had gone in far enough: oxygen was making its way to Crépin Vandégueux's lungs. One thousand four hundred and fifty-five, it was a continuous flow, the air entering and leaving with a truly unpleasant cavernous sound, the sibilant shrieking of a ghost in a third rate horror film.

At one thousand five hundred and thirty three I'd summarized the situation for a nurse miraculously arrived at the nurses' station, who in her most suave voice called "Code 99" into the hospital loudspeakers.

At one thousand six hundred and ten I'd hurriedly collected my things and was leaving without awaiting the outcome.

At one thousand seven hundred and seventy-six, a large deputation of medical personnel was quickly making for the resuscitated patient's room.

I stopped counting at six thousand nine hundred and forty-one, outside, in a cold as sharp as my knife. I wiped the other party's blood into the snow. First I thanked all those documentary teams who have been striving for years to present rather unsavoury (but oh so educational) surgical interventions on TV. Trembling, I then awarded myself a first prize in all categories of skilfulness: I'd had a fifty per cent chance of killing Crépin Vandégueux. Why exactly did I do what I did? I still don't know the answer except that I didn't have time to think. And only later did I think that I'd missed out on my true career, because a surgeon has the means to heat her home over the Christmas period, while a writer doesn't. A writer warms herself on her sentences.

I hope that very shortly Chapter Two's ghost will be kind enough to snuggle up close under the covers.

◆

LET'S FORGET ABOUT GHOSTS. Cats' ghosts. And all the other ones too.

Nothing.

There's nothing happening.

I'm freezing.

Outside.

Inside.

The abortion was a year ago now, night for night.

I don't see Violette any more; she told me that since she was born in Algeria, she's not isothermic enough to risk going out; the winter even attacks her nerves.

I dreamt that my brother Vincent hanged himself on the shower head in my bathroom, and that I brought him back to life *in extremis*.

There's no explanation for that nightmare because he and Valériane are in the Azores together.

(And so I'm doubly short the bowl of steaming soup she used to make me at lunch time, doubly because friendship keeps the heart warm, after all).

Furthermore, Valériane and Vincent are so

much in love that it's made a few of the sutures from my past come undone.

In short, I'm whining.

I can't take it any more.

I'm experiencing the tundra of the soul, much worse than the other, geographic, tundra.

Readers, I beg you to console me, grant me the Caribbean of kindness, an Africa of goodness, a super-nova of human warmth, relieve me of this black hole I'm foundering in, help!

(And thank you.)

(Thanks in advance.)

◆

ALL RIGHT, ALL RIGHT, all right. Let's get a grip on things. The bomb hasn't gone off yet (although it is proliferating), Reagan has retired (although Bush...), the Imam Khomeini is on the verge of joining Allah (although his heir...), my computer hasn't broken down yet (although the mouse is limping a bit and being capricious), I haven't got cancer yet (although there's a pain in my back, on the left, when I cough), I may get a child to take care of (although I have to get full marks in the

Social Services inquiry), and today, because of the greenhouse effect, winter is telling a colossal lie and appearing in its gentlest guise without even a cloud around its neck: a fake spring in the middle of January, there's no way I can spit on that. So that's enough whining and bleeding hearts!

Besides, as the young Belgian poet, Alex Millon, recently wrote me, "I know no better chemotherapy than writing!" So, let's get to work.

◆

(I KNOW WHAT I have: I'm somewhere around page 100 of my manuscript, and anyone who writes will confirm that page 100 is a crest, to climb up to, or throw yourself off of, or smash against.)

Remember Jacinthe? the one who is Rocky's and Anémone's mistress? the one who's blond as a morning in July? She took me out to her cottage this week; that's what she calls it, a massive understatement because it's actually a stately residence, with tawny woodwork, pastel futons, a fireplace and ready-cut firewood in a box; and beyond the windows, a lake, immense and uninhabited, except by fish (relaxing for a few more months under at least fifty centimeters of ice). Contemplating all this sky, (transparent, at least to the naked eye), and this expanse of snow, (undisturbed, except by rabbits), listening to this silence, (or rather this peaceful uproar), brings on prayer. So I, the atheist, prayed to the sky and the snow and the lake water, and even the fire on the hearth. I called on them very strongly, "Take me, take my pain and my fear, let me become a cat in your gigantic skirt, stroke me between the ears so I can find my purr again; better yet, turn me into a nut, crack my shell, swallow me in one gulp, digest me till I disappear, I can't go on, I don't want to go on, I give up, I don't know any more, I never did, oh you, who are almost immutable, truly powerful, wise, and calm, help! There. I hand myself over to you. My burden is now in your hands."

And then the miracle occurred: after my prayer I slept fifteen hours without a nightmare. True joy!

◆

NOTHING TO REPORT today. Except that out front, on the sidewalk totally pitted with ice, I was brutally thrown from the saddle, without even being astride a horse. Nothing really special in that, it's a regular occurrence of the season. But here's what was phenomenal: a driver stopped on the cross street to see if I needed help. I emphasize this trifle because he was a good twenty meters away, and if he'd continued on his way I wouldn't have been the least bit angry; but with a mere touch on the brakes, this man contradicted all the ranting and raving about the Me generation, urban dehumanization, modern egotism, and all the rest. However, since it's not physical help I need, I gave him the thumbs-up sign. I wasn't lying: today, in the face of his gladiators and underhanded retiarians, Winter, the dictator, granted me a little respite.

◆

VALÉRIANE CAME BACK from the Azores with skin like melting caramel, and the kind of gaze I imagine on angels in seventh heaven. We went to have supper with her sister, Dahlia, in a Portuguese restaurant not far from here (since it was twenty-seven below zero, we didn't feel inclined to stroll too far). The place was empty. The owner lit a fire in the massive fireplace; then Paco, Juan and Paulo, the three *fado* singers with mandolin and guitar, sang us a few songs till my heart got even more tangled. We even sang along, nothing very serious, just some *la-las* in the choruses, but the winter, the slush, poverty, pollution, the bombs, torture everywhere in the world, Palestine, South Africa, my sore throat, sore soul, sore being, all that faded for a few hours. Everything black evaporated.

As we left, Dahlia whispered the following riddle in my ear, "Do you know why when you throw pebbles into water, they make rings?" I said no. With a complicitous smile, she said, "Because they never forget anything."

I agreed, as you can well imagine: memory is a confused compass.

◆

THIS MORNING I read in the papers that due to extremely low tides, there's no water in Venice. The gondolas have run aground in a blackish mud, shiny with too many used condoms and all the other unidentifiable, smelly stuff. I feel like the Serenissima. Do cities have nightmares? Do souls celebrate Mardi Gras once a year?

◆

OH! THE SOCIAL SERVICES inquiry is drawing closer: a social worker is on her way to check me out. In exactly seventeen hours and thirty-nine minutes. So I've suddenly become an artist of the vacuum cleaner, a virtuoso of the feather duster, a star of the floor rag: this morning, at three minutes past nine, no one would have recognized me or my house. I spent the whole night and a slice of dawn washing and polishing the floors, the walls, the mirrors, the bathtub, the sinks, the toilet bowl, the tables, the refrigerator, the stove, the cupboard doors, the dishes, the four wastebaskets and eleven ashtrays, and then I transformed myself: I

removed my make-up, took off my studded
leather bracelets, flattened out my punked-up
hair and gummed it down with some left over skin
cream; from a box in the closet I dug out a
harmless little dress,[12] ironed and starched it, and
put it on along with a pair of nylons that were
hiding in a bottom drawer. Taking even more
precautions, I hid all my asthma medication, my
cigarette papers and the incense, and I was ready:
my home and I were ordinary, banal, normal.
Phew!

The meeting with the lady from Social Services
went very well. She was around retirement age,
kindness shimmered in her eyes, I felt that she
must have grappled with quite a number of dis-
gusting injustices (I can always identify the war-
riors of hope). I had to confess everything, my
childhood, my mother, my girlfriends, my former
boyfriends,— why I loved them and why I left
them— my work, my sources of income (I didn't
expand too much on that subject), how I felt

---

12. A yellowish-grey polyester outfit that Marguerite, who never
gives up, bought me twelve years ago just in case I got a sudden
attack of conformism.

about raising children, in short, I talked non-stop for four hours and she took notes. I carefully avoided telling her what I was writing about. And please note that I didn't light up a SINGLE cigarette! I no longer work as an actress, but it's like sex or bicycling, you never forget how. Now don't go thinking I lied to her— it wouldn't have done any good anyway, I'm sure that woman could easily see through the slightest fib—, no, my acting talent came in handy for the way I talked to her: I was ordinary, banal, normal, and I'm sure the lady from Social Services didn't for a moment suspect my true harridan nature.

◆

(I'M SO TIRED. Discouraged. I could sleep for a hundred years. A kiss wouldn't wake me up: I never miss it these days anyway. I could sleep for a hundred years. It's been raining since yesterday.)

Oh! Excuse me. I completely forgot you for four lines there. Actually, I'll be honest: it's been quite a while since I thought about you at all. Every now and then I've had a twinge of remorse, but to tell you the truth, it just gave me a thicker skin. Self-preservation. So here's what's happened: you've only turned one page, and through a trick of literature, six years have gone by. Excuse me for ignoring you for such a long time, but a major geological fault, a maximum crevice opened up in the minimal landscape of my life, in short, I haven't even had half a minute for you. And don't think I'm back for good now (unfortunately for me). It's Monday morning; I have till Sunday evening to tell you everything. That's when François-P. will be back from his excursion with

Caroline, Lucie, Odile, Josepha, Jesula and our
most recent child, Annie.

So, I've got seven days and six nights to bring
you up to date on everybody, and give you a whiff
of my very real love life.

The abyss, or rather the first of the series, was
Caroline, the eleven-year-old little brunette that
Social Services placed with me. It's a well-known
fact that a child will change your life, but an
eleven-year-old who has been a victim of incest
since age seven at the hands of her father, her
uncle and her brother, that's an instantaneous
abyss. I remember our first day together, we were
both equally intimidated, but she was tangled up
tight in the most dismal misery, the most distress-
ing fear, and the most thunderous unhappiness. I
leapt into the drop, my sleeves rolled up, my heart
ready.

Good thing I had a number of rehearsals for the
famous play, *The Torture of Insomnia*, behind me,
because for the first month I didn't close my eyes.
I thought about Caroline all the time, I'd go watch
her sleeping, on her back, her arms over her eyes,
her feet set flat on the mattress, and her knees
spread wide apart, it depressed me totally. Poor

kid without a childhood, shattered and frag-
mented. She reminded me of the evergreens in
northern Quebec, abused by winter, by acid rain
and bud worms. But by the end of three weeks,
Caroline would accidentally call me *maman*, quite
by accident, I swear. Six months later, she was
chirping away under the shower in the mornings,
and I bought a bunkbed to accommodate her and
the next one, her (almost) sister, Lucie.

Please don't think I'm a saint: the profit in
happiness-capital was immediate. I never stopped
asking myself: am I doing this for her or mainly
for myself? I'd become a foster home, but the heart
of the home was Caroline. You love a child, and
the child loves you back, never before had it been
so uncomplicated to get heaps of affection. Still,
let's not tell lies: sometimes the size of the task
completely weighed me down: I was labouring in
a trench. Caroline, the trench.

But she always figured out ways to pay me back.
A drawing, a good grade at school "just for you,"
or her little hand wiping away an old tear, the
power a child has over pain is amazing.

(I'm completely worn out. I can't swallow de-
feat. In love, I could resign myself, I often did. But
not now, the mash left in the sieve is just too
gummy, it won't go through.
    It's been drizzling all day.
    I'd like a brown Siamese cat with a squint. A cat
I'd call Melon-Skin. Who'd rub up against my feet
while I wrote. While I wrote... I wonder whether
my gang of sweethearts has managed to keep a fire
going? The fall's already so chill.)

With Lucie, a *dolina* aged ten, it was more
arduous. Her mother, a topless dancer, had aban-
doned her, and Lucie was in her seventeenth
foster home in five years. Lucie, or Maximum
Mistrust, the nickname I gave her— a bad habit I
have— didn't talk. Not to Caroline. Or to me. Iron
determination. Cast iron silence. Caroline
couldn't get over her tenacity. M-M had been with
us ten and a half weeks when Valériane lost her
baby, three days before it was due.
    I should add that my brother Vincent and my
dear neighbour had decided to endow their pas-
sion with a soul, a body and a first name. And

during the eight months and twenty-seven days of her pregnancy, no fedayin of happiness was more dazzling.

But that afternoon, while we were doing homework, Valériane came through the door of our shared balcony. With a face like an earthquake.

The baby was dead before it was even born.

The floodgates of tears opened noisily for Valériane, Caroline and me, to Maximum-Mistrust's amazement. Thirteen days later Valériane was still crying, the sun still avoided our street, and my youngest (almost) daughter still hadn't said a word. I sent her over to Valériane's with this note: "Dearest neighbour, could I please borrow your jar of mayonnaise, I don't have enough for our chicken and alfalfa sanwiches tonight. Thanks." Three-quarters of an hour later, Maximum-Mistrust still hadn't come back, but over the phone Valériane told me not to worry. Her voice was a tiny bit less distressed. Then Lucie came home. For the first time she undid her long blond braid herself. She told me matter-of-factly that she'd played mama and baby with Valériane, but that Valériane had been the baby, and she, Lucie, had rocked her and sung to her till she fell asleep. She

added that every night she'd have to take care of
Valériane. As long as she hadn't recovered from
the death. I said yes, as you can well imagine.

(It's still drizzling, endlessly. I feel in exile in my
house. I just had a look in the bedroom of my
(almost) progeny. Only Annie's corner is in per-
fect order, which worries me, it's too tidy: for a
little girl of nine it seems maniacal. I dreamt that
my shrivelled hands fell off like two dead leaves.)

When you've been up in the mountains, and
you've made your way through a dangerous
gorge, climbed a rockface and negotiated a sharp
crevice, after you've caught your breath on a
deceptively anodine plateau, have you ever
blandly thought that now everything would be
simple, there would be no further surprises, only
to have a blow of the ice axe reveal an unsuspected
chasm? Four months after Lucie came, Odile was
that chasm. It was January, a calm night of full
moon. I remember I was making yogurt and
thinking about how placid the moon was when

the doorbell went, at four in the morning. It was Odile, a friend of Lucie's, a little girl from the neighbourhood we'd never really noticed. That night, red-haired Odile had two black eyes, and the bottom of her nightdress was still damp with blood. She was holding her left arm, broken. Stammering, she told me her father had beaten her unconscious; then, probably thinking she was dead, he'd strangled her mother and put a bullet in his own head. A chasm, I can assure you. With the follow-up— police, inquiries, funeral, and Odile's placement with us— our little home caved in under the maelstrom. Oh, we tried so hard not to forget the direction of the light. For months Odile sobbed with Lucie, with Caroline, with me, all alone, at night, during the day, at school, at the Portuguese grocer's, building a snowman, watching TV, skipping rope, and inevitably it was massively contagious, we sobbed with her. In their frequency and volume, her nightmares surpassed those of anybody else in the house. Odile, my Trembling-Fountain. Then, little by little, time softened the tragedy.

I mustn't leave out anyone. My mother, Marguerite, has set out to study philosophy. She can hardly sleep any more. She confided to me that rather than just barely sensing the troubled waters of daily life, she was now for the first time unfolding her spirit far above the melee. And Violette, she's remained my good, sharp-tongued fairy. Right now, her younger daughter, Gentiane, is studying alto clarinet at the Conservatory, and Mélisse is in pediatric nursing at the university. The most striking event in Violette's life occurred three years ago. In the furnace room of her apartment block she discovered an archangel. Actually, no one has ever seen him, but if you leave a beat-up old bike down there, a broken toaster, or an exhausted hairdryer and wait for two or three days, you can be sure the thing will be repaired. However, it doesn't work with broken hearts: you can't ask too much of archangels.

Nevertheless... I have to admit that when Violette told me the story of the archangel in the furnace room, I went down there for an hour to read *The Room of Miracles*, by François Charron, one of the most beautiful collections of poetry I know. In a voice that resonated strangely off the pipes, I did several recitations of the poem "I can't imagine wanting it different":

I can't imagine wanting it different
the taste of your tongue praying on mine.
I can't imagine wanting it different
the lovers' contact that refuses the
question and wraps them in wrinkled
sheets, worn sheets, sheets without
a memory of imposed walls. [13] (...)

I thought it might please the archangel and he might take notice of my unhappy little self. And two days later ... François-P. Beauregard came into my life! I'm not lying, I swear! Irrefutable proof that archangels, at least the ones from furnace rooms, are sensitive to poetry...

It was May 15. Caroline, Lucie, Odile and I were walking down Saint-Denis. We are very European, and prefer to do our shopping every day. The first spring days had been wet and more than brisk, but that day a voracious breeze was covering us with torrid kisses. Lucie had put on my leather jacket, Caroline was decked out in my thirty-seven studded bracelets, and Odile was

13. François Charron, *La Chambre des miracles*, Les Herbes rouges, Montreal, 1986

wearing my old Stetson, which was too big for her and came down over her eyes— if you're going to open your heart, there's no reason not to open your closet. We'd just come past the Michel Tétrault gallery where an opening was in full swing. The three kids were stopped short by the picture in the window. We went in, and in front of a gigantic painting entitled "Vertigo of the Eyelids," I was struck by the syndrome Stendhal once described. Imagine a forest clearing in which a family of fifteen people is assembled, everyone from the baby to the grandmother. All of them are painted in the purest hyper-realist style, but the faces look as though they've been wiped away with a rag. All the faces, except the grandmother's. I was floored, and waited feverishly for her to start singing a lullaby in her nuanced voice. I was shaken from head to foot, while my (quasi) brood commented on how the title might be connected to the work. I didn't notice François-P. step up. He started talking to my tourmaline, my opal and my carnelian. When I was finally able to detach myself from my fascination and turn toward him, I almost passed out, or through, or under, or more exactly, fell over into the cigarette butts that littered the floor. François-P. is red-haired, red as the moon before an eclipse, as a holiday sunset, and his hair cascades down to his waist. That day he had his hair undone, and in my distraction I thought he was a reincarnation of Thor himself. My (quasi) descendants immediately noticed the effect that François-P. had on me, and they went to great lengths to introduce me: I was not their real mother, but I loved them like a real *maman*, in other words, I was an open-the-brackets-AL-MOST-hyphen-close-the-brackets-mother, and what did it matter anyway that I hadn't had them, since I was the one who tucked them in at night, and the one they could hold on to as much and as long as necessary if they had nightmares? François-P. had to chuckle at such a barrage of explanations. He shook my hand, he was the creator of all these paintings, could he see me again? Lucie replied that we didn't live very far away, that I was always at home, and Friday evening we always made pizza and each time there was some left over, if François-P. wanted, he could come to eat next Friday, okay? François-P. agreed, and Odile, who is in charge of my wallet, gave him my business card. I remember that for some time, I felt as though my face and my body had been whipped by a pair of colossal wings.

When we got home, the girls were overflowing with contentment and predictions. Odile said that with my masculine haircut I was a good match for François-P. and his long, flowing hair; Lucie thought François-P. looked as though he wouldn't hurt a spider— a stroke of luck, when you think of our colony— and Caroline, just a little acid, made fun of me— the colour of my ears, my cheeks and my neck.

I remember I burnt my left hand four times during the four days preceding that Friday. François-P. came to supper with a bouquet of tiger lilies, immaculate spirea and a cinnabar red rose. All of silk. "For you to keep forever. Like me, I hope," he murmured. Solemnly, very solemnly.

I'll get to the point. For a month we sat on the stairs and seduced each other, unaware that upstairs, behind the door, my sweethearts were quietly spying on our developing idyll. It had been several millenia since I'd heard anyone older than sixteen say "I love you," so you can understand the upheaval my whole being underwent, in the middle of the staircase, in the arms of François-P.

But THE crucial moment was bounding toward us, the moment of bodily truth, when you make it or you break it. I had to warn the girls. Not about the nature of sexual relations— Caroline had already informed them— but about the fact that at the moment of pleasure, women, sometimes men, and I in any case, could cry or bellow or growl, yell their lungs out, even howl. That was something Caroline didn't know. I told them several times, "Don't be afraid, don't call the police, I can get pretty noisy."

I'll deliver the goods in bulk, there's no time to be perfectionist: oh my love, François-P., his milky skin, cunnilingus with his hair spread like an opulent fan over my hips, our bucking, his mane whipping through the half-light and the fireworks going off in my room, my memory wavering, my flesh wavering, losing control of everything, of myself, my identity, my past, the other men before him, forgetting everything, misfortunes and courage and childhood and fears, no longer knowing whether I was the furious sea or the resistant rock, the wave or the undertow, I tried to avoid crying out by biting into the edge of his hand, but some situations are impossible, infinite, and then his hand was bleeding, oh, his unflinching erection, oh miracle of prayer felicity supplication unexpurgated ecstasy, oh François-P., your keen vigilance over the flights and then the falls of my orgasms, your pianissimo, your glissando at the speed of light, our lips slipping with kisses, our thighs foaming with my juices, and finally the spicy aroma of your sperm, and above all our gazes mingling in the first light of day, when we could feel that the exodus was over, and that finally we had reached the land of satiation. The land where love is finally sown.

(I let myself get carried away. I'll have to hurry. Six days have gone by already. I hope I'll have time. At least for the essentials. But how do you choose, can happiness be summarized in trifles? It's still drizzling, the sky is anthracite and cold. Why do I have this tenacious feeling that I'm dying in a slow freeze? I am in love, I am loved, so why is there this hollow in my heart, why this void that wounds me: what is it?)

A little less than two years ago, François-P. told us that he wanted children too. The discussion was short; he planned to adopt. Briefly:
a) A cardiologist and a sterile neurologist had paid the twenty thousand dollars required to adopt a set of Haitian twins from the orphanage Notre-Dame-du-Perpetuel-Secours in Petit-Goave. The old missionary from Quebec who ran the establishment, Sister Jeanne d'Arc Chalifoux, was so happy not to have to separate her eight-year-old twins that she "neglected" to let the doctor couple know that Josepha and Jesula limped. So the cardiologist and the neurologist refused to take the children, which proves that you can be a heart or a brain specialist without having any yourself.
b) Josepha and Jesula landed with us in November, a dreadful, polar November. Stupefied by the snow, they exclaimed in unison, "Neige-saa, vinn pou non, bon Dié, a la tracas pou malhéré!"[14] They started on

---

14. Freely translated: "Godawful winter!"

accelerated French and we began with Creole
101. I nicknamed them Vesuvius and Etna
for their exceptional dynamism.

That winter there were numerous electricity
breakdowns, due to Hydro-Québec's outmoded
equipment. Each time, Caroline, Lucie, Odile,
Vesuvius and Etna took joyful refuge in our bed.
With the added discomfort of poverty's very
pointy bones, it was just like the subway during
rush hour— not that it mattered much— waking
up was always a light-hearted affair anyway.

(In five weeks, Caroline has to go back to her
real mother, because her brother has moved to an
apartment of his own, her uncle has emigrated to
Vancouver— a city he doesn't deserve— and her
father died in prison under suspicious yet easily
explained circumstances when you know even a
little about convicts and their holy hatred for that
kind of criminal; in short, Caroline has to go back
to her real mother because from now on, she will
be safe there. You should see how elated she is, it
would break your heart.

And now... let me tell it all. This is what upsets

me the most. François-P. has kept on painting. While I've stopped writing. Six years already. So if my calculations are right, I've spent two thousand and ninety-one days, or fifty two thousand five hundred eighty four hours far away from you, unable to write... Could that be the reason for my pain?

The sun's rising, viscous and very tentative. I'll have to hurry, they'll be back in three hours.)

Two weeks ago, Annie, an earthquake of unimaginable proportions, aged nine, arrived.

A scourge. An attack of nerves every hour. In permanent conflict with reality. Which she rejects. And opposes with all her strength. Remarkably intelligent. But devoted to revolt. And destruction. Here is a partial list of the damage she did within the first seven days and seven nights: Caroline's comics were in tatters, Odile's flute in pieces, Lucie's records smashed, the only photo Josepha and Jesula brought with them from Haiti was in shreds, François-P.'s paintings were full of holes, my collection of dolls systematically wrecked. The scourge operated at night, once she had exhausted us with her tumult during the day. We tried everything: discussion, humour, caresses, periods of isolation, threats, without result. The scourge probably wanted to test our capacity for love. After seven days and seven nights, the place was in ruins, physical and psychological ruins. As a last attempt, François-P. suggested a trip into the forest with the girls, without camping equipment, or food, or even a match, just a survival knife. In its handle are a compass, a fish-hook, a harpoon, a metal trap wire, and a piece of something or other that strikes sparks when you rub it against a dry rock. Still, one survival knife pitted against the savage immensity of the Quebec forest and in night temperatures of minus four Celsius is not a lot. We thought that faced with survival problems, the scourge would perhaps agree to collaborate. In order not to die. My (almost) tribe gallantly accepted the experiment. I was exempt from the expedition, for reasons of existential unease dating from well before the arrival of the scourge.

(You should see the state of the house today: stacks of unread newspapers still on the doorstep, twenty-four empty milk cartons lined up on the counter, a tumulus of cigarette butts in each of the eleven ashtrays, my bedsheets completely disheveled and the bathtub horribly ringed by a number of successive baths. My hair is drab, my skin just superficially clean, I look decrepit, but I'm happy. Because I'm writing. Because once again I've leafed through my old *Petit Robert*, my paperback *Littré*, and the dear old Paul Rouaix I inherited from papa. I can't say it's been easy to get back to the keyboard after a six-year absence, it's not that simple, but oh, the intimate and secret pleasure of unearthing unknown word-gems from the pages of my dictionaries! It is only here, amid the lines, with the words, with you, that I survive. That I'm revived, and survive. And live. Yes. That's it. Writing as an ultimate gesture of love. Which is what I've been depriving myself of. But no longer.)

(In what condition will my tribe arrive presently? Famished, but pacified?)

(I have such a longing for my sister in exile in Paris. In Paris.)

(I was seven years old. It was raining that morning. I loved the rain because then I could put rubber galoshes over those damned orthopedic shoes. On the way to school, I amused myself kicking showers of water into the puddles. A gust of wind caught under my big umbrella and lifted me off the ground for two seconds. I think I will feel nostalgia for those two seconds till the day I die.)

Montreal
January 8, 1988 - February 1, 1990

ACKNOWLEDGEMENTS

The author [15] would like to thank:

— for their love and all their inspiration, her female friends Agnès, Johanne, Julie, Flora, and Hélène;

— her mother Gracia;

— Johannes Brahms, Leonard Cohen, Paolo Conte, Miles Davis, Pierre Flynn, Patricia Kaas, and Richard Séguin, whose music and songs accompanied the writing of this novel;

— le ministère des Affaires culturelles du Québec, for a subsistence bursary for four months;

— le ministère de la Sécurité du Revenu du Québec, for having assured her survival for six months (while harassing her).

15. A NOTE ON THE AUTHOR

Actor, union official, filmmaker, and journalist Anne Dandurand was born into good company in Montreal in 1953. From 1973 to 1988, she performed on stage and more often on television for Radio-Canada (most notably in plays by Strindberg and Sartre). In 1978, she was elected President of the Committee on the Status of Women of la Fédération des travailleurs et travailleuses du Québec (Workers Federation of Quebec). She has written and directed two short films, *Ruel-Malenfant* (1980) and *Le rêve assassin/Death of a One Night Stand* (1981). From 1982 to 1987 she was a journalist and art columnist for *Châtelaine, La Vie en Rose, Québec Rock,* and *Montréal ce mois-ci,* among others. In 1987-88, Radio-Canada broadcast *Rachel et Réjean inc.,* for which she co-wrote story and dialogue with her twin sister, Claire Dé. In 1982 Dandurand and Dé published a collection of short fiction on which they had collaborated, *La Louve-garou* (La Pleine Lune). In 1987 Dandurand published her first solo collection of short fiction, *Voilà c'est moi: c'est rien j'angoisse (journal imaginaire)* (Éditions Triptyque). Her second, *L'assassin de l'intérieur/Diables d'espoir* (XYZ Éditeur), appeared in 1988 (also published in English by Véhicule as *Deathly Delights*), followed by *Petites Ames sous Ultimatum* (XYZ, 1991). In 1989 she received *Le Grand Prix de la nouvelle pour la jeunesse,* awarded by le Salon du Livre in Montreuil, France. Dandurand is presently editorial director of the mystery novel series *Alibis* (XYZ Éditeur). Her sole passion is writing.